"Why, Ca ~~to see how~~ **you?"** Grant asked fiercely.

"I don't know." She took one last, forbidden taste of the feel of his thigh beneath her palm, then forced her hand away. "But we're playing with something dangerous and we have to stop."

He lifted one hand to her neck, brushing it down the slender column with a feather-light touch, then stroking his thumb over the hollow where her pulse thrummed in a give-away rush.

She cursed herself for the immediacy of her response, for the wildness surging against her will. "You shouldn't do that."

He bent his head closer, and for one heart-stopping moment she thought he would kiss her. "How can anything so good be wrong?"

She didn't have an answer.

"Have I ever told you how I feel whenever our eyes meet?" he murmured.

She shook her head, pulling away as he caressed the curls at her nape.

"No? Well, did I ever tell you how I wish I could bury my face in your hair?"

"No," she whispered.

"You have no idea the number of times I've imagined tasting your mouth, devouring it, kissing you until you whimpered for more."

"Please," she begged. "Please stop."

"I won't force you, Cammie. But you are fighting yourself, not me. Like it or not, you do want me. And we both know it. . . ."

WHAT ARE *LOVESWEPT* ROMANCES?

They are stories of true romance and touching emotion. We believe those two very important ingredients are constants in our highly sensual and very believable stories in the *LOVESWEPT* line. Our goal is to give you, the reader, stories of consistently high quality that may sometimes make you laugh, sometimes make you cry, but are always fresh and creative and contain many delightful surprises within their pages.

Most romance fans read an enormous number of books. Those they truly love, they keep. Others may be traded with friends and soon forgotten. We hope that each *LOVESWEPT* romance will be a treasure—a "keeper." We will always try to publish

LOVE STORIES YOU'LL NEVER FORGET
BY AUTHORS YOU'LL ALWAYS REMEMBER

The Editors

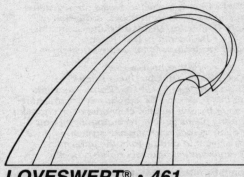

LOVESWEPT® • 461

Olivia Rupprecht
Taboo

BANTAM BOOKS
NEW YORK · TORONTO · LONDON · SYDNEY · AUCKLAND

TABOO

A Bantam Book / March 1991

If you would be interested in receiving protective vinyl
covers for your Loveswept books, please write to this address
for information:

Loveswept
Bantam Books
P.O.Box 985
Hicksville, NY 11802

ISBN 0-553-44107-8

Published simultaneously in the United States and Canada

PRINTED IN THE UNITED STATES OF AMERICA

OPM 0 9 8 7 6 5 4 3 2 1

One

"Put it in that way," he instructed patiently.

"But it's too big," she insisted. "It'll never fit, Grant."

"Then we'll make it fit. Now look, Cammie," he said reasonably, guiding her hand with his. "All you have to do is hold it . . . just so. Work it back and forth, real easy now. Make sure there's plenty of lubrication. That's a girl."

"Grant," she muttered, "it's too tight."

"Just a little resistance," he murmured close to her ear. "And I know just how to take care of that."

She shrieked in sudden pain. "Dammit, Grant! You shoved it in. And just look. I'm bleeding."

"Well, hell," he shot back, "it wasn't working the other way, and at least we got the damn things connected." Grant dropped the WD-40 and the wrench next to the dryer vent, where the metal tubing now fit snugly. His victory was quickly forgotten as he jerked Cammie's hand up for closer inspection. "You *are* bleeding. C'mon, I'll take care of that."

"I think you've done enough already," she grumbled, and he felt the distinct urge to kiss shut her lushly pert mouth. "And besides," she added saucily, "*I* was always the one patching up *your* scrapes. With as much practice as you gave me, I'm probably better off doing it myself, little brother."

Grant pulled himself up to his full six-foot-three height and towered over her, drawing his shoulders back so his muscles flexed over a darkly tanned bare chest, which gleamed with sweat. It was hot as Hades, thanks to a late September heatwave that had descended on Austin like an electric blanket stuck on high.

He held out his hand and she took it. Grant told himself he should be used to this by now—this current, this one-sided jolt, this . . . this physical want he'd nursed since the day Cammie Walker had moved into his parents' house and taken up residence in his heart. He'd been eleven; she'd been fourteen. Seventeen years hadn't changed anything.

"Little?" he repeated dubiously. "I passed you up size-wise a long time ago."

"That's right." She laughed, then swatted his behind before turning on her heel to stride toward the bathroom. "Even then you were too big for your britches."

Wanna find out just how "big" I am for my britches, Cammie? Grant gritted his teeth, holding the words back. *Just how big I get every time you slide your fingers up my side to tickle me, the way you did when we were kids? Wanna find out just how hard I am right now, after one of your little torture treatments with your hand patting my rear?*

Grant wasn't smiling as he trailed after her, watching the sway of her sweetly curving hips in cut-offs, the firm and taunting rise of her tush as the hint of a cheek peeked beneath the frayed denim. Her blond hair was a tangle of shoulder-length curls, and more than anything he wanted to comb his fingers through it, to brush her hair the way she'd let him once when she had baby-sat him and Trish, his *real* sister.

Cammie was rummaging around in the medicine cabinet when he reached the doorway. Leaning in, he noticed her makeup, her curling iron, and hair things scattered over the vanity. Stockings were draped invitingly over the towel bar. He spotted a pair of black panties thrown into a white wicker basket in the corner.

Entering the small room, Grant grasped her wrist as she splashed water over her hand. He rubbed his thumb gently over the small cut before dabbing on some peroxide.

"You know, Cammie," he said quietly, letting a subtle but distinct insinuation flavor his tone, "I'm no more your real brother than I am a kid any longer."

Cammie reached for a towel, and her arm brushed against his chest, immediately tautening his abdomen. She efficiently patted the cut dry, her impish grin firmly in place as she looked up at him with wide, clear eyes. Eyes the color of the sea, and just as changeable. Feeling himself slipping, he let it happen, going down and then under, drowning in their aquamarine depths. He'd quit fighting the undertow a long time ago.

"You were *never* a kid, Grant. I can still see you peeking out the window the first day your parents brought me home—looking at me with those somber brown eyes of yours. Even your teachers said your book reports were like something put out by a congressional committee. And remember how your coaches kept saying you had lots of potential, if only you didn't think so hard and could let your reflexes—"

"Thinking's gotten me a long way in life," he cut in, in self-defense. "Three patents and two in the making aren't too shabby for a guy my age."

"Of course not," she said, and covered his hand in affection. "I'm proud of you, Grant. Everyone in the family's proud of you. You're a wonderful inventor."

He brought her injured palm to his mouth and pressed his lips to the soft flesh. He always found lots of ways to touch her—and he supposed the pretext of platonic caresses was better than nothing.

"I'm sorry you got hurt," he murmured. "I never want to see you hurt."

She kissed him soundly but chastely on the cheek, and his jaw locked tight. His lips compressed in equal measures of frustration and desire and fury.

"You're sweet, Grant," she whispered. "The sweetest brother a girl could ever ask for."

Dammit, wake up and look at me, Cammie Walker. I'm not your brother. I never have been. I'm a man. A man who wants to get out of this prison of family ties and this farce of a relationship. I'm a man who's in love with a woman who can't see beyond a screw-up of fate.

"I'm *not* your brother," he repeated, this time more assertively.

"Of course you aren't," she agreed with an innocent smile, while he fought the urge to mold his thighs to hers and prove just how un-sweet he could be. "But you might as well be. Now, get those cute little buns out of here so I can get ready for work. Got to look my best, you know. Can't have the six o'clock news with a ratty-looking anchor."

"You look great, just the way you are," he assured her, letting his gaze travel leisurely from her head to her toes and back. He fixed her with a challenging stare.

"Get outta here, you big lug," she said, turning his simmering once-over into a joke. "Go on." She pushed him out the door with a hand between his shoulder blades and another pulling at the waistband of his jeans, pretending to throw him out. "Scat, before I shove you into the tub. You need a bath before you go on your weekend prowl even worse than I need a man to help me fix whatever else can go wrong around here."

She booted him out with her foot planted firmly in his backside, then slammed the door shut with a girlish giggle. He noticed she didn't lock it. Of course not. After all, he was just family.

Grant leaned against the door frame, listening as she sang a bawdy ditty he'd taught her sometime when he was thirteen and she was sixteen and the family had gone camping. Trish hadn't come along, and he and Cammie had had the pup tent all to themselves while his parents took the big canvas on the other side of the fire. He remembered their staying up half the night exchanging naughty jokes and snickering into their sleeping bags so the grown-ups wouldn't hear.

He remembered Cammie falling asleep first and the way he'd studied her by the dim light of the dying fire. He remembered stealing his first kiss, his heart pounding like a drum as he'd furtively brushed his lips over hers. She had murmured in her sleep and snuggled closer to his sleeping bag.

He remembered how cautiously, like a thief stealing something priceless that he could never claim as his own, he had draped his arm over her shoulders and brushed the hair away from her face. He'd had his first wet dream that night. Cammie had the starring role.

Grant heard the sound of her zipper sliding down. Closing his eyes, he imagined peeling the tight-fitting shorts off her body, and her lacy silk panties right along with them. The sound of water rushed in the background, and his mind toyed with the image of Cammie sinking naked into his private hot tub . . . and into his arms.

"You need a bath before you go on your weekend prowl even worse than I need a man . . ."

That's what she'd said. And what was he, chopped liver? No, wait. A little brother, right? As usual, the lightly spoken quip flailed him, stinging and more hateful than any insult she could ever dish out. It made the futility of his unrequited love all the more frustrating. All the more infuriating.

Grant pushed away from the door as he heard her splashing water over her body. The body that was so sweetly familiar and yet so forbidden.

He slammed the front screen door open and was storming out to his sexy imported sports car—that for all Cammie would notice was a four-door Ford—when he realized he hadn't locked the door.

Turning back, he flipped the latch, ever careful for her safety. He stalked back to the Porsche and folded his oversized frame into the front seat, then revved the engine with a vengeance.

Squealing out of the old brick driveway, he decided that Cammie was right. He did need a bath. And he was on the prowl—for the occasional easy lay he resorted to when he couldn't stand another night of the gnawing, ceaseless appetite he had for a woman as close as a sister and as distant as the stars.

Tonight was one of those nights. He'd stop for a box of condoms, maybe pick up a decent bottle of wine.

Then he'd pick up an old bedroom pal who expected nothing more than a good time—Cecilia or Julie or Brandy. After he caught the six o'clock news.

The night had a purpose, and that purpose should be in full swing no later than ten. When he gave in to the urge, he liked it right about that time. Tangling in the bed, or skin slick and limbs meshing in the spa, it didn't matter. There was a television both places.

He'd make sure it was on. Just so he could tell himself that while she did the ten o'clock news, Cammie could see what she was missing.

"We'll be right back with an update on today's fatal collision and footage of the accident that took the lives of a local family. This and more to follow. Stay tuned."

The floor manager signaled that the camera had ceased to roll, and Cammie took several deep, steadying breaths. She didn't need to look at the notes she was gripping to know she had a case of the shakes.

"Hey, Cammie. You all right?"

"Sure, Russ. I'm fine." She gave her co-anchor a weak smile. "I just hate covering these accident reports. They really get to me."

"I know." Russ Aberdeen reached over and gave her hand a quick squeeze. "Want me to stand in for you on this one? I'll give Jack the word and get the cameras and TelePrompTer in my direction."

"Thanks anyway, but I'll handle it. Goes with the territory, big guy." Besides, she silently added, it was how she stood up to the old demons. They never went away and she'd quit running years ago.

"Cammie," Jack, the studio manager, called, "you've got some sweat on your upper lip. Quick, Tino, get some powder on her before the countdown."

"Roger." Tino rushed over to quickly pat dry Cammie's flushed forehead and around her mouth. "Lights warmer than usual, Cammie?"

She forced a halfhearted smile for an answer and muttered, "Thanks, Tino," just as he moved away and Jack signaled with the countdown.

"Three . . ."

You can do it, she told herself. You've got to do it. Damn, quit shaking, would you? A hundred thousand viewers are tuning in. They'll all know if you screw this up.

"Two . . ."

The internal command went unheeded. She could feel her vocal chords contracting. Get your act together, she frantically ordered. It's your job. Just a job. Not your life. Not your family. They're gone.

"One." Jack pointed sharply at Cammie.

"Today a fatal collision between a Mack truck and a station wagon claimed the lives of a local family, leaving five people dead . . ."

Cammie drew on every ounce of professional know-how she possessed to maintain her outward control. Her eyes met the camera as she struggled to keep her self-protective shield firmly in place. If nothing else, she was grateful the footage began to roll as she recited the worst part of all. . . .

"The Rawlings family, on their way to a picnic, were traveling approximately sixty miles an hour when a tire punctured on the truck, causing the driver to lose control and jump the median. Danny

Rawlings, his wife, Cindy, and their three children—Jayna, Christy, and Robert—were pronounced dead after rescuers . . ."

Cammie breathed deeply of the humid late-night air as she leaned against her monster of a car. She didn't care that the old El Dorado wasn't glamorous. It was at least ten times safer than that fast and dangerous death trap Grant drove like a bat out of hell.

Glancing at her watch, she saw that it was eleven on the nose. She hadn't wasted any time getting out of the studio. Now that her weekly stint was done and she had the weekend off, she wanted to put the cloying memories in the past where they belonged and clear her head. Life was too precious. She didn't want to spoil a minute of it.

"Cammie, glad I caught you."

She turned as she swung open the door to her car. "Got a news flash for me, Russ?" she asked with feigned humor, determined to pull herself out of the depression pits.

"No," he said, matching her light tone. "I just wondered if you might be up for a TGIF celebration. Some friends of mine are throwing a bash out by Lake Travis that should last till dawn. Thought you might be game."

"Thanks, Russ, but no thanks. I've already got plans." She was prepared, the excuse ready on her tongue.

"What kind of plans this time, Cammie? I'm starting to think you're giving me the brush-off. Five turndowns in a row makes a guy start to wonder."

"Okay, Russ. Here's the deal. One, I never date my co-workers."

"So if I switch channels, you'll give me a chance?"

"Don't be silly. You know you've got the next-to-best slot in Austin."

"True. But something tells me that the lady with the prime-time smile wouldn't go out with me whether we worked together or not. What's reason number two?"

"Two is . . . none of your business. I keep my personal life to myself."

"So I hear. I guess there's someone special, huh?"

She looked away. She didn't owe Russ or anyone else explanations . . . which was just as well, since she spent a lot of energy avoiding facing the facts about her less-than-ideal love life.

"Have fun, Russ." She got into her car and shut the door, then rolled down the window. "And thanks for the invite. Drive safe and I'll see you Monday."

"Sure thing. Watch out for the crazies on the road."

"I always do," she assured him with a "click" of her seat belt and a farewell wave.

As she drove away, Cammie glanced at Russ's fading image in her rearview mirror and breathed a sigh of relief. Keeping men at bay got awfully tiresome after a while. But after three broken engagements in twice as many years, she was taking some time off from the singles scene.

Maybe she'd still be dating—since she did like to get out—if this last breakup hadn't been so awful. All the engagements had ended for pretty much the same reasons, but the latest ex-fiancé, a high-powered broker, had been brutally honest. The fight alone had left her glad they had called it off.

"You never let anyone get too close, do you?

he'd said to her that last night. "*No wonder your relationships never work out. Turns out the leading lady of the airwaves is nothing but a fraud. Yeah, she looks like a woman a man couldn't get enough of . . . and that's just about right, isn't it, doll? But maybe that's because you're already giving the best of yourself to that brother you can't quit talking about. Grant this, Grant that. If he's so perfect, maybe you deserve each other.*"

"Grant," she sighed into the darkness, then shook her head. Turning on a local FM station, Cammie wondered if maybe there hadn't been a smidgen of truth in her fiancé's verbal attack. She found that she did compare other men with Grant, and ultimately they all came up short. Besides, she loved Grant, more than anyone else in the whole world. Even more than his parents, who were the closest thing to a mother and father she could ever have.

Grant was the brother God had given her for the one she'd lost. He could always make her furious or make her laugh, or more often than not simply glad to be alive. He was her soul mate and her secret keeper, and she would fight to the death to protect him.

Only Grant didn't need anyone's protection, she reminded herself. He'd made that clear a long time ago. Sometimes, especially in the years since he'd graduated from college and established himself independently, she wondered how well she knew him, *really* knew him.

He had changed, and more than physically. Oh, sure, he was still genius material, quite the young, new inventor, making the family proud as peacocks. And he was fun, still teasing her the way he always had. Just like today, when he'd pretended to give her a leering once-over with his Romeo eyes that dropped the girls dead in their tracks.

She wasn't sure when it had happened, but Grant had grown up. He was a man—a ladies' man, a man's man. His own man. Too bad he was the closest thing she had to kin. He was the kind of man a woman could fall in love with.

Cammie realized she was idling the old El Dorado in front of Grant's house. They lived a good ten miles apart, but her car seemed to drive there on automatic pilot half the time. It had been rough that night, covering the accident. She didn't want to go home and face the empty house alone.

Since Grant's car was in the driveway, indicating he was home, she walked up the uneven ledges of the lushly landscaped lawn. The front door was unlocked. That meant he had to be around somewhere. Alone? She hoped so. She needed his company. No demands. No need to keep the conversation running. Just the closeness they shared.

Letting herself in, Cammie called his name. No answer.

"Grant?" she said again, moving cautiously in the direction of his bedroom. The door was open, the lights on. The big platform bed was made. Furniture and gym equipment were all in place. No scattered undies were lying around.

Cammie realized she was strangely glad of that. As ridiculous as it was, as platonic as their relationship was, she still found herself not wanting to share Grant.

She thought she heard a familiar sound track playing on the other side of his "think tank" room—the big den where he did most of his mental gymnastics, sketching ideas like crazy. If that was where the music was coming from, it meant he was in the hot tub.

Backtracking, she padded softly over the Indian-weave rugs that were scattered across the wood-planked floors of the front hall. Just one of the many projects they had taken on together—they'd sanded, then polished and laminated until the oak gleamed and their knees ached.

She passed beneath the familiar massive ceiling beams and beyond the masculine leather furniture she had helped Grant pick out and arrange in his living room. Edging through the kitchen she spent as much time in as her own, she heard the music more clearly.

Cammie paused beside the French doors that led onto the redwood deck, where she could hear the spa gurgling and churning about fifteen feet away. One door was partially open, and she grasped a polished brass knob, ready to make her entrance.

"Gra—" The syllable died on her tongue while her body froze.

She hadn't opened the door more than a few inches when Grant stood up in the hot tub, spot-lighted by the moon's glow, the water roiling and surging around his hips. His chest was broad and covered with a thick mat of hair. It was the same chest she had rested her head against too many times to count . . . but somehow, the way the light caught and played against the thickness of muscle and sinew, he seemed suddenly more pagan than fraternal.

Cammie ordered herself to let go of the door-knob. As she did, he moved with a quick, lithe grace, hoisting himself naked onto the deck, close enough for her to see each delineated line of his broad back, his thighs, his buttocks.

His silhouette arched when he stretched and reached up, as though embracing the star-studded sky. He shook the water from his dark, unruly hair and laughed seductively.

Then he pivoted. Cammie's throat went dry. She told herself not to look, to move away, that this was wrong.

Wrong or not, for a moment she couldn't budge. She was mesmerized and stunned and . . . no, she couldn't be. It wasn't possible . . .

Without her conscious consent, Cammie's gaze moved over his body, memorizing the alternately rough and smooth textures of hair and skin, the planes and angles and indentations of his physique: Grant—majestic, beautiful, and erect in all his masculine glory.

As she backed away from the door, Cammie's breath caught sharply while an ache gripped her deep inside. Escaping to her car, she acknowledged the unbelievable truth, as undeniable as it was taboo.

Grant had been fully aroused. And even now, running as fast as her legs could take her, trying to forget the image she couldn't forget, so was she.

Oh, Lord . . . *so was she.*

Two

Grant squinted against the midmorning rays piercing through the overcast sky. He hoped it rained. It would suit his mood. After his romp the night before, he should be feeling pretty good about life in general and himself in particular.

He didn't. He felt disgusted and as empty as a discarded corn husk. Brandy was a heady and sensual woman, but come the morning light he didn't want to look at her. Or himself. He'd forgone shaving just so he wouldn't have to face the mirror.

Shifting the white bag, from which emanated an aroma of hash browns, bacon, and scrambled eggs from a neighborhood take-out joint, he knocked twice on Cammie's door and waited. When she didn't answer, he fished in his pocket for his key and let himself in.

Judging from the drawn curtains and the fact that the only sign of life was from the fish swimming in her aquarium, he figured Cammie was still sawing logs. Alone.

Once when he'd let himself in, she'd been in a

state of half-undress with her fiancé—he thought it was fiancé number two. He'd wanted to commit an act of homicide, as if it were *his* right and not her fiancé's to have access to her body. Somehow he'd gotten out of there without resorting to a scene, and settled for drinking and partying himself into oblivion that night.

He never knew why, and he didn't believe in questioning a higher deity about miracles, but for some reason she had broken the engagement the next week. And since breakup number three, she hadn't been seeing anyone else.

Yes, he thought it was safe to assume she was alone.

Alone and, he hoped, sleeping naked. As he tapped on her half-open bedroom door and called to her softly, Grant knew he wasn't above stealing a peek of any flesh that happened to be uncovered. Hell, he'd had nothing but stolen kisses and stolen glances to get him through, from puppy love to an adolescent crush, to . . . now. The real thing.

When she didn't answer, he pushed the door open with his foot and crossed to the edge of the bed. Her hair was a mass of tangles and half covered her face; one bare arm was thrown over her head. Her mascara was smudged and her lips were slightly parted as she breathed evenly and deeply. Her chest rose and fell with each breath, her breasts swathed with a smooth dark sheet, but beckoning him nonetheless.

Grant swallowed hard and shut his eyes, trying to adjust his act to suit the situation. This was just a brotherly visit, the Saturday brunch they usually shared since the family was thirty miles away and neither had a steady.

He had to remember that she didn't take him seriously when he was at his most serious. That was always dangerous—things like yesterday's overtures. If Cammie ever guessed how serious he really was, there was no telling how she would react. Chances were, it would create a breach between them. He couldn't bear the thought of giving up even a fraction of her affection, no matter what form it took. Brotherly love was better than no love at all.

Forcing his body to ignore its instincts and his psyche to assume the role she had cast him in, he waved the paper sack just beneath her nose, back and forth, until her head subtly swayed in the direction of the tantalizing fragrance.

"Mmmm," she murmured groggily, still more than half-asleep.

Keep it light, he told himself. Keep up the "just family" routine. Keep the invisible emotions hidden so she doesn't trip over them and stomp all over your heart.

"Oh, Sleeping Beauty," he sing-songed, "it's your wake-up call. Come and get it."

"Mmmm," she groaned again. "Go away . . . I'm sleeping . . ."

"So I noticed. I heard you cutting Z's all the way to my house. Anyone ever tell you that you snore? Or that you sleep with your mouth open and have a tendency to drool?"

"Buzz off, Grant," she mumbled, and rolled over, covering her head with a pillow. "You're a pain in the butt."

He chuckled and made a neat dive to the other side of the mattress. The old iron bedsprings squeaked and groaned beneath his weight. He wrestled the pillow from her grasp and plumped it up behind his back.

Cammie's eyes opened suddenly as he kicked off his shoes and stretched, before proceeding to dig into the take-out sack. He smiled and winked as he waved a piece of bacon back and forth like a pendulum.

"You are getting sleepy," he murmured hypnotically. "Slee-py . . . sleee-py . . ."

"Grant!" she squawked. "What are *you* doing here?"

"What do you mean, 'What are *you* doing here?' I'm eating breakfast. The same way I do every Saturday. If you don't get up, I'm gonna eat yours too."

"But you can't!" she said frantically.

"Of course I can. I'm doing it. See?"

Cammie looked unusually disoriented, he noticed, especially as she clutched the sheet tight and high about her neck, her eyes avoiding his.

"How did you get in?" she demanded.

"I used my key. What else?"

"And you're on my bed. Get off my bed. Right this instant."

"Jeez, Cammie, what's with you? You got a case of PMS or something? Want me to get you a Midol out of the bathroom, or—"

"Out!" she ordered. She let go of the sheet long enough to give him a push and point what looked suspiciously like a shaking finger in the direction of the door.

"If you wanted some coffee, all you had to do was say so," he said reasonably while his gaze immediately followed the descent of the sheet. She had on a T-shirt, but he could see the thrust of her breasts, the jut of her nipples.

Grant forced himself to look away and gather up the scattered Styrofoam containers before he had yet another raging fire to douse.

He stopped at the door and glanced back. Cammie was looking at him with an odd kind of confusion—almost as though she had been awakened by someone she'd thought was a stranger and just now realized it had only been he.

"Are you okay, Cammie?" he asked, his brow furrowed with concern. Then he remembered. He'd been in the middle of some pretty heavy foreplay, but he'd been sensitive to her every move, every nuance of impression.

"Cammie . . . Last night . . . I'm sorry, I forgot. You must be upset. Want to talk about it?"

"What?" she croaked. Her gaze darted around the room before settling uneasily on him. "Last night? What about last night?"

Cammie was acting awfully strange, he mused. He propped an elbow on the door frame and studied her curiously. The sack dangled from his hand and for a split second he almost dropped it—the split second that he thought she looked at him differently than ever before. With a spark he recognized as unadulterated feminine . . . interest. Not interest, more than that.

Desire.

He must have imagined it, though, he decided, because whatever he thought he'd seen was instantly replaced by something else—guilt, maybe? That didn't make any sense either.

Grant shook his head, deciding he was so deep into his own obsession with Cammie, he was starting to project his emotions onto her.

"You know," he said, "last night. The accident report. You covered it at ten, remember?"

"*I* remember," she retorted sharply, "but I'm surprised that *you* do."

"Of course I remember," he said tolerantly, even more confused by her belligerent attitude. "And I know how upset you get when you have to report on them. Especially the accidents with kids and

families. I just wanted to make sure . . . Hell, I
don't know what I wanted to make sure about.
Just if you wanted a listening ear, or a shoulder to
cry on. I've got both whenever you need them,
Cammie. You know that. I thought maybe now was
one of those times."

"Grant . . ." Her face softened, then she smiled
uncertainly. "I'm sorry, Grant. I didn't mean to
snap at you. You, of all people. You're too special to
me, and I should realize, more than anyone, not to
take the people I love for granted. Ever since
Justin died—" She swallowed hard, glanced away
and then back. "You know you've always been the
closest thing to a—"

"I know," he sighed. "A brother."

She nodded and held her hand out to him. He
dropped the sack on the bedside table and sat
beside her, taking her hand in his, kissing the soft
palm, then laying it over his heart. He was glad his
shirt was partially undone. It gave him the excuse
to press her hand to his bare skin without seeming forward or out of line.

His eyes met hers, with empathy, with compas-
sion, with love, though he was careful not to
betray the deeper, more urgent kind of bond he
ached to forge, the heavy pulse rushing between
his temples, expanding inside his chest, and culminating painfully and unsatisfied—*never* to be
satisfied—between his legs. She did all this to him
with no more than the lightest caress of hand to
chest.

Unexpectedly, her fingers spread beneath his
and pressed, sinking into his skin and threading
through the thick wiry hair before tentatively brushing his nipple. His breath caught. He thought his
heart might pound through his ribs, if he didn't
have a heart attack first.

Her caress was subtle but distinctly sexual, and he wondered if she had any idea what she was doing to him, or if she was aware of the intimate implications in so small an act.

He scrambled out of the cloak of disbelief, of longing that had descended over his brain like a fog, scanning her face, her eyes, searching for some kind of message, some signal to tell him he wasn't dreaming for once, that at last she had seen him for what he was, recognized him as the man he had become.

"Cammie . . . ?" His voice was hoarse, thick.

He saw it again—the flicker that he could only pray was desire, a smoky haze in the depths of her troubled eyes, banked and cautious, but holding the promise of fire if he could stoke it just right.

But so quickly it was gone, overlayered by confusion, struggle. And then a look of disbelief and disapproval, as though she couldn't believe what she had just done, but knew that she had and was horrified.

She quickly let go without actually jerking away and clasped her hands tightly together, staring at the lace-curtained window.

"You'd better go eat your breakfast," she said quietly. "Go on, you. Git, before it's cold."

"Cammie." He touched her cheek, and this time she did jerk away.

"And make some coffee while you're in there, okay? I think I'm still asleep."

"I think you're just waking up."

He stroked his fingers through her hair, but she grasped his wrist and held it tight before thrusting his hand away.

"Cammie, don't—"

"No, Grant. *We* don't. Not you. Not me. Understand?"

"No, I don't understand. Talk to me, Cammie. Talk to *me* for once. Not some kid who grew up years ago. I want to talk about what just happened, about—"

"It didn't."

"It didn't what?"

"Happen. It didn't happen, Grant."

His eyes slitted, his lips barely moved. "You're a liar and you know it."

"Stop it," she hissed. "Stop it now. Nothing happened. *Nothing.*"

"Coward."

He reached out to grasp her arms, but stopped himself. She would only shove him away. So he got up, aching and elated and frustrated and more determined than ever to make it the way it should be with them—now that he knew there was something to build on. He'd seen the chip in her facade. He'd hammer at it until she succumbed.

Stopping at the door, he let his gaze trace her shape beneath the sheets, and this time he had the pleasure of knowing that she most definitely took him seriously.

The way she huddled and drew her legs close beneath the flimsy covering told him so.

"I'll make some coffee," he said smoothly. "Meet you in the kitchen . . . *sis.* You don't mind if I call you that, do you? I mean, since we both know nothing happened."

She flinched, obviously rattled and upset. He was perversely glad. Maybe he should have destroyed her lofty opinion of him a long time ago, peeled away the image she clung to and given himself a chance at building a new one.

"Oh, and by the way," he added casually. "I had a message on my machine this morning from Mom and Dad."

"Mom . . . and Dad?" She gulped the words out and cast a furtive glance in his direction.

"Yeah. My—our *parents* want us to join them tomorrow for church and Sunday lunch. And they have a couple of extra tickets for a football game. Thought we might like to come along. I called them back and accepted. Hope you don't mind."

"Mind?" she echoed. Her voice sounded very small, and she was kneading the sheet with her hands.

Grant raised a brow to let her know he'd noticed. He leaned against the door frame just a little longer to assure himself he really did have the power to unsettle her. Once he was satisfied that she was definitely breathing in an erratic, shallow pant, he moved away.

"Coffee's on," he threw over his shoulder.

"Grant."

He turned.

"I . . . don't think you should come into my bedroom uninvited again."

"Wouldn't dream of it," he assured her. "I can wait for the invitation."

He turned on his heel, his mind spinning, his body still rushing, and his heart thumping like mad.

He'd thought brotherly love was better than no love.

He'd been wrong. One touch, one very provocative touch, was all it had taken. He needed her love the same way he needed to breathe.

Cammie pretended to concentrate on the magazine, the pages fluttering with the Porsche windows half-down. She only wished Grant's leg wasn't so close, the well-honed muscles bunching beneath the smooth fabric of the gray suit he was wearing to church.

She'd probably seen him in it ten times that year, but for reasons she did not want to explore, she'd never noticed until now how well the tailored coat accentuated his broad shoulders, or how the white dress shirt and dark silk tie set off the healthy bronze glow of his skin and the strong angle of his freshly shaven jaw. But worst of all was the way his pants fit snugly around his lean waist and hips, and tightened just enough at his thighs when he sat down to remind her of the pagan god she had seen surging out of the water and arching toward the night sky.

"Want me to roll my window up?"

Cammie started at the sound of his voice. The voice that was deeper, more gravelly, and far more assertive even in casual conversation then she ever remembered it being. Like the voice of a stranger . . . and yet the most familiar voice in the world.

"No," she said without looking at him. She didn't want to be reminded of the way the wind was ruffling his unruly hair. "No, but you can slow down."

"Sure. Anything you say, Cammie."

He shifted down, and his hand brushed against her silken hose. She jumped before she could stop herself, and silently cursed the instinctive reaction. Grant had touched her a million times, but ever since yesterday's unreal and yet all too real encounter, nothing was the same with them. Not even a casual and possibly intentional brush of his hand against her leg.

She concentrated hard on the article, then realized she'd read the same paragraph three times and didn't have the faintest idea what the article was about.

She was still too disoriented to form a coherent thought—disoriented and appalled by her voyeuristic arousal. Even more, she was disturbed about and unbelieving of the shocking turn their relationship had suddenly taken.

Grant had overtly and without hesitation let her know that his feelings for her were adult and not brotherly in the least. But how could that be possible? How could he have changed overnight—or had he? Had she been so blind, so entrenched in the familiar, that she hadn't looked beyond the surface to see the obvious?

She didn't know, nor could she explain her own inexplicable and sudden awareness of him as a man. It was horrible and intriguing and mind-shattering . . . but most of all, unacceptable.

Grant was her brother. Not by blood, but they were linked with their souls, with familial bonding and ties, with holidays and shared joys and sorrows. They had been closer than a lot of natural siblings she knew, always seeking the other one before going to anyone else for advice, for support, for love and laughter.

Right now she was so confused and upset, she needed Grant more than ever. He was her best friend and she craved his advice, his insight to sort out this crazy mess.

Yet just when she needed him so badly, they couldn't talk. That was the most devastating blow of all—losing him this way. She missed her brother and she wanted him back.

She risked a fleeting glance in his direction, and he intercepted her, his eyes sober but alight with something she'd never seen before yesterday. That something teemed with masculine prowess, with emotional depth and longing, with a proprietary and distinctly sensual intent. The wind whipped through his hair, and she caught the faint hint of cologne, a scent that was clean, woodsy, intoxicating.

He'd worn it for years, but he'd never before smelled so incredibly good, so good that she wanted to bury her face in the crook of his neck and breathe in deeply.

Her throat constricted and she looked quickly away. Her head swam; her heart hurt so bad, she wished she could weep.

They could never go back, but they could never go forward. This was the second brother she'd lost, and somehow the pain was worse as an adult than as a child.

Maybe because this time she knew the depth of her loss.

Grant pulled into the church parking lot, throwing a casual wave and a happy greeting in the direction of their parents, who were waiting for "the children" just outside the majestic old Methodist church.

Cammie automatically reached for her door handle, grateful to get a little distance from Grant, though at the same time she dreaded facing Mom and Dad under the awkward and inappropriate circumstances.

Grant caught her wrist before she could open the door. "Hang on. I'll come around and get you."

"I can open it myself," she protested, trying to keep things as normal as possible." I always open my own door . . . Bro."

His face hardened at that last word. His grip subtly tightened.

"Stay put," he ordered. "The rules just changed."

"Grant, you've got to stop behaving like . . ."

"Like what? C'mon, Cammie. Say it."

She looked away in time to see their parents strolling toward the car. She let go of the handle.

"Okay, Grant, you get your way this time. Open the damn door and do it fast. Mom and Dad are almost here."

"And we wouldn't want to cause a scene, right? We know how they hate to see us squabble." He narrowed his eyes, then his gaze lowered, momentarily to linger on her lips before he abruptly looked away.

Seconds later he was striding around the car and opening her door. Cammie didn't offer her hand, but he took it anyway and helped her out.

"What's the matter, Cammie?" he asked, his voice low. "Your hand's awfully damp, and I do believe you're shaking."

She was spared the necessity of a reply by their mother.

"Hey, kids, you made it on time for a change. Grant, you didn't speed to get here, now did you?"

"Hi, Mom," he said, letting go of Cammie's hand to give Dorothy Kennedy a big bear hug and a sound kiss. "And no, I didn't speed. Cammie made me drive five miles under the speed limit."

"That's my girl," Edward said as he embraced Cammie in his loving, paternal arms. "Make him toe the straight and narrow. You know we count on you to keep him out of trouble."

"Oh, she makes it hard for me, Dad," Grant said, "But that's okay, 'cause I know she's really soft as butter inside."

While Edward clasped his son's hand and laughed heartily, Cammie fought the distinct urge to slug Grant. She might have, if Dorothy hadn't kissed her cheek.

"Cammie, sweetheart, I'm so glad to see you. You're so pretty up on that TV. Dad and I have everybody we know watching you. Oh, and I almost forgot. When we get home I've got some material I found that'll be just beautiful for that dress pattern we picked out for you last month."

"Great, Mom," she said with an enthusiasm she was far from feeling. "I can't wait. And talk about pretty, I love your new outfit. Did you make it?"

"Why, sure. Got to keep my fingers busy. The Good Book says, idle hands are the devil's workshop."

"The preacher's right on that score," Grant said, sliding Cammie a mischievous grin. "I try to keep mine as quick and clever as possible."

Dorothy smiled proudly. "I know you do, son. You're just so gifted and imaginative. I declare, the Lord must have been feeling generous the day you were born."

"I think so too, Mom. He gave me an extra portion, and a man has to be thankful for that." Grant nodded amiably as he draped his arm around Cammie's shoulders, looking amazingly sweet and innocent as he brushed his fingers back and forth against the bare skin of her upper arm.

"So, son," Edward said, "just about got that special fishin' pole worked out for Audrey? That's all she talks about every time she and Trish come to visit."

"It's almost done. I ran into a few hitches, but I've about got it worked out. I wouldn't be much of an uncle if I let my only niece down, you know."

"Oh, dear," Dorothy said. "Church must be starting while we're standing around gabbing. I think I hear the organ."

Grant nodded. "I think I hear it too. Maybe we should go on in. When the organ's touched just right, it's a beautiful thing to behold."

"That's a fact," Edward said, hooking his arm through his wife's and leading the family toward the sanctuary. "Come on, kids. Time to sing some hymns, give some thanks, and get rid of the week's guilt. Or maybe get some more, depending on what the good reverend decides to preach."

Cammie hung back just enough so Dorothy and Edward were a good ten feet in front of them. Edward was middle-age handsome, and Grant favored him; Dorothy was a maternal version of a young Judy Garland. It was all too easy to see the similarities between them and their son. But looking at their trusting faces and being enfolded in the unlimited bounty of their love—something she'd always associated with Grant as well—Cammie decided she had grossly misjudged her adoptive brother somewhere along the line.

"You should be ashamed of yourself," she hissed as his hand fit snugly in the small of her back. "All those innuendos in front of your parents."

"Innuendos?" he repeated incredulously. "What innuendos, Cammie? I was just going along with the folks. And you do make it hard for me, you know."

His seductive chuckle was interrupted by a grunt of pain as her elbow connected with his ribs.

"I hope the preacher heaps all kinds of guilt on your head today," she said between clenched teeth.

"Not likely," he shot back. "I don't feel any remorse for having my prayers finally answered. Took Him long enough. After seventeen years I was beginning to think He'd disconnected the line."

"That's blasphemous, talking like that."

"No, it's not. It's honest." He stopped short as

their parents reached the open and welcoming doors of the church, from which the organ music spilled out. "Hear that? It's the doxology. When we get in there I *am* going to give thanks. Because whether you can accept it yet or not, you're struggling against the tide. Come to me, Cammie," he whispered, "and rest your soul upon the peaceful shore."

The sun wreathed the back of his head in a halo of light. Her eyes locking with his, Cammie couldn't begin to sort out the conflicting emotions and sensations ricocheting between her head and her heart. Nor could she control the sensual awareness that had lain dormant for so long, but now blossoming with unnerving speed.

Glancing at Mom and Dad, who were smiling and signaling them to hurry, Cammie felt a wave of guilt, the certainty that they would be hurt and mortified by a romantic liaison between their adopted daughter and their son. They'd consider it illicit—at best; a sin, perhaps.

All these things hit her at once, and had the effect of an A-bomb being dropped inside her head and exploding down to her toes.

She gulped in a steadying breath of air and tossed her head indifferently.

"Lay my soul upon the peaceful shore?" she repeated on a laugh. "Really, Grant, you must have an inflated opinion of yourself. A sandy beach or an overused hot tub deck comes a lot closer, if you ask me."

He regarded her shrewdly when she mentioned the hot tub, and Cammie wished she could take that part back. But then he laughed.

"Leave it to you to keep me on the straight and narrow," he said, taking her arm and leading her to the entrance.

"I know, I know," she muttered. "But that's okay, because I'm soft as butter inside."

"Are you?" he whispered, his breath warm and fragrant, wisping seductively against her ear and raising the hairs on the back of her neck.

Cammie drew in her breath, thankful the usher was prompt, but not so relieved when she saw it was a full house and he was leading them to a crowded pew.

If there had been any way, she would have maneuvered herself between Mom and Dad, but unless she made an issue of it, she was stuck next to Grant. Stuck next to this man she was beginning to believe was more a stranger than an old and comfortable friend.

Sharing a hymnal with him was sensual and emotional torture, his voice vibrant but a little off-key while his hand touched hers beneath the well-worn binding. As if that weren't enough, they were sandwiched in, so that Grant had to drape his arm behind her back, leaving her no choice but to stay locked by his side, hip to hip, thigh to thigh. For all their Sunday clothes, she was beginning to feel like Eve, naked and tempted by the forbidden fruit.

The most difficult part of all was saved for last, when the good reverend asked everyone to join hands with those sitting next to them while he said a parting prayer—which turned out to be an unusually long one.

Mom's hand was as warm and loving as ever on her left. But when Grant's fingers laced with hers, Cammie couldn't deny that a current passed between them that transcended time and propriety and the entrenched boundaries. She felt like the old skin of their friendship was being shed while something brilliant and new grew in its place.

Then he moved his thumb, taking the hidden access to her sensitive and moist palm. He stroked it back and forth, tracing a slow, deliberate pattern, turning the simple act into the most heady and forbidden indulgence of the senses she'd ever experienced.

He squeezed her hand, then repeated the strokes, and she realized he was sending her a message—a game they had played as children, one scratching out symbols while the other tried to decode the secret words.

She felt the distinct strokes, long, then short . . .

Her eyes opened and immediately locked with his as he repeated once more:

The I . . .

Followed by a heart . . .

And ending with the letter *U*.

Three

"Here, let me get that." Grant managed to lean into Cammie, brushing his chest against her bare arm as he snagged the jar of freshly preserved tomatoes from the top shelf, which was just beyond her reach in the walk-in pantry.

"Thanks," she said, her voice strained as their hands brushed when he passed it to her.

Grant let his fingers linger for a luxurious moment, then broke the contact. Before she could hide the truth, he saw the proof, the small frown of disconcertment. Of disappointment.

Oh, it was good. Hell, it was wonderful, fantastic, exhilarating! Just as electric as the shared bond that had leaped and surged between them less than an hour ago. He owed the reverend. That long, drawn-out closing prayer had had some miracle magic, and Cammie hadn't been able to disguise her response. She was too transparent to begin with; Cammie couldn't lie her way out of a paper bag. Besides, they could read each other as if with ESP, and both of them knew it.

"Hurry up, kids," Dorothy called from the adjoining kitchen. "We need to change clothes and eat so we're not late for the game."

"Coming!" Cammie wheeled around, then froze as Grant grabbed her hand. Her gaze riveted on his firm fingers as he curled them into her soft, warm flesh.

"Sit with me at the game," he murmured.

She swallowed hard before darting a furtive glance toward the kitchen, where they could both hear Dorothy stirring something on the stove and humming to herself.

"I don't think that's a good idea," she whispered.

"Why not? You never minded sitting with me in the past."

"That was before . . . before . . ."

"Before, what, Cammie?" he demanded huskily. "Before you found out I'm no brother and we've got something brewing between us that's a lot more potent than affection?"

"No!" she said sharply. She jerked away from him, and the jar slipped from her hold. It crashed loudly, glass and tomatoes splattering on the linoleum floor, his shoes, and her hose.

"Uh-oh! Did something break?"

They heard Dorothy's scurrying steps just before she appeared in the pantry doorway.

"It's nothing," Grant said, smiling. "Just a case of butterfingers. Can you get us a mop and a towel, Mom? I'll clean the mess, but we'll track up the kitchen if we don't wipe this off first."

"Be careful of the glass," she admonished before heading to the utility room.

"Damn you, Grant," Cammie whispered. "See what you made me do? Now stop this nonsense before anything else happens."

"I didn't make you do anything. You tried to run

from me all by yourself. And if you think I'm going to stop this 'nonsense,' you can forget it. As far as I'm concerned, we're just getting started."

For a moment they locked gazes and wills. Grant's lips were compressed in determination; Cammie's trembled slightly in spite of her sharply spoken warning.

"You're crazy," she finally said in a tight voice, and looked away.

"You're right," he said quietly, then traced a single fingertip along her delicate jaw. "Crazy about you."

Her gaze flew to his, and she mutely shook her head in denial.

"What are you so scared of, Cammie? Me? Or yourself."

"Here's the mop." Dorothy rounded the doorway just as Grant withdrew his lingering touch.

"Thanks, Mom." He reached for the mop handle. "Cammie, grab that towel, would you? You can start with my shoes. I'll take care of the floor."

"That's fine," Dorothy said. "If you've got it under control, I'll get back to the stove."

"Oh, it's under control," Grant assured her as she turned to go. "I've got it *all* under control."

"Hang on, Mom," Cammie blurted a bit too loudly. Grant could hear the edge of desperation in her voice. "I'll come help in the kitchen."

"Don't bother. Just help your brother."

Grant smiled in satisfaction while Cammie nervously bit her lower lip.

"Hear that, Cammie? Mom says you need to help me. I can always count on Mom to be in my corner."

"Bastard," she whispered.

"Don't tell Mom that. She's under the impression I was a planned pregnancy. And I don't think Dad would take to me belonging to the milkman." He chuckled as her hands twisted the towel, as if she wanted to strangle him with it. Glancing down at the floor, he added matter-of-factly, "I'll start mopping. You can start with the shoes."

"Clean them yourself."

He let go of the mop to catch the towel she hurled toward his face.

"I swear," he grumbled good-naturedly. "Here I thought I was doing you a favor by mopping, and I get stuck with double duty. Oh well." He sighed. "If you insist."

Oblivious to the glass crunching beneath his heels, he bent down, sliding one hand over the side of her leg before running his palm up her calf and holding her firmly behind the knee.

"What do you think you're doing?" she asked, her voice almost strident but carefully quiet.

He looked up into her startled, flushed face—flushed because she was reacting exactly the way he intended, whether she liked it or not.

"Just getting the tomatoes off your hose," he said calmly, then studied her shapely legs at close range, just as he'd longed to for years. Lord, it was almost too good to be true . . . touching her this way, feeling the fine tremble as she responded instinctively to his caress.

Cammie abruptly leaned down to stop him, and almost lost her balance when he tightened his grasp on her leg. She automatically caught his shoulders, and he slowly raised his head.

Their faces were only inches apart. He could see the sudden dilation of her eyes, could hear the catch of her breath. Their gazes locked. The air fairly crackled with charged intensity.

"Careful," he whispered. "If you fall, it'll be on me, and believe me, I'm already nursing an edge that's cutting me deeper than any of this glass ever could."

"I . . ." She wet her lips, and he clamped down the urge to capture her tongue with his before it slipped back into the inviting recess of her mouth. "I'd rather do it myself, Grant. Give me the towel. Please."

"Not a chance. And unless you like to live dangerously, I suggest you hang onto something besides me."

Breaking the visual contact and ignoring the silent plea in her voice, he smoothed the towel up, down, around, managing to rub a lot more in than off. Cammie released his shoulders and straightened, her movements jerky.

"Kids, are you almost done with that, or do I need to come in there and—"

"That's okay, Mom," Cammie called back, a distinct waver in her voice. "We're almost through."

"Okay, but hurry up. Dinner's on."

"Be right there," she said, and tried without success to extricate her leg. She pushed at Grant's shoulders. "Stop it. That's enough."

"Oh, no, sweetheart. It's not nearly enough."

Cammie's calf muscle tautened and quivered. He kneaded it insistently, expertly, then pressed his lips to just above her knee.

"Grant!" she gasped.

"Much better," he murmured, then released her with the greatest reluctance and swiped at each of his shoes. He stood quickly, before she could flee, and caught her hand. It was wonderfully damp, and he took enormous pleasure in its unmistakable tremble.

"Look at me," he commanded gently.

She hesitated, then tilted her head up. Her eyes were wide, and at least a little scared. But the joy of it was, he didn't think he scared her half as much as she scared herself. There was no disguising the dark flare in her eyes. Her unwilling arousal was hot as fire, and as impossible to hide as his own. His body was all but pulsing in a turbulent, rushing beat.

"You go help Mom," he murmured. "I'll take care of the rest of this."

"I'll take care of it," she insisted. "*You* go help Mom."

"Why?"

"Because I don't want to face her."

He noticed that Cammie looked a little ashamed, and he hated that. Resented it beyond measure. Sparing her no quarter, he glanced down at the front of his trousers, where his fly was straining in blatant protest to the internal pressure.

"Better you than me," he said without a trace of shame.

She blushed a vivid scarlet, then managed to gulp out a single, "Oh."

"Oh, yes." Before she could break away, he brought her hand to his mouth and pressed a kiss into the center of her palm. His fingers circled her wrist, and he could actually feel the leap of her pulse.

Knowing time was out, he took comfort in that single unspoken sign and ordered himself not to be greedy. Not to jeopardize the hard-won victory by an irrational act of emotional hunger and physical lust.

Placing the towel in her palm, he folded her fingers around it and made himself let go.

"I'll put this away," she said in a pitifully vain attempt at normal conversation, obviously reluctant to leave the haven of the trap he'd created in exchange for their parents' company.

"Good idea." He smiled, tenderly tucking a stray curl behind her ear and grazing a finger across her lobe.

"Then I'll go help Mom," she added before turning resignedly in the kitchen's direction, carefully stepping around the litter of glass and vegetables.

"Cammie."

"Yes?" She stopped but didn't turn to face him.

"Sit with me at the game?"

She hesitated, and his hand clenched tighter around the mop handle.

When she agreed with a single, stilted nod of her head, he relaxed, silently rejoicing in the triumph.

She took another step and he said again, "Cammie."

"What now?" This time she whirled to face him, her hands wringing the towel. "How can you expect me to go in there and act normally when you keep dragging this out? I'm going to have to give the performance of my life as it is, Grant."

"You forgot something." He managed a smile in lieu of a satisfied smirk and reached up, latching onto another glass jar. "The tomatoes."

It was dusk when they gathered beside Grant's car. Dorothy hugged Cammie close.

"We're so glad you could come and be with us today. We miss you kids, you know."

"I miss you too, Mom," Cammie said, returning the embrace.

"What about me?" Edward teased as he kissed her on the cheek. "Don't I get a mention?"

"You too, Dad." She hugged him tight to prove it.

"I hope you had a good time today," Dorothy said. "You seemed anxious about something, Cammie. Is everything all right?"

"Oh sure, Mom," she lied around a mouthful of

guilt. "I'm fine. And the game was great. Almost as good as your cooking."

Great? she repeated silently. Torture. Unbelievable, skyrocketing, "if he touches me or looks at me that way again I'll go out of my mind from wanting more and what in God's name am I thinking?" torture.

"I know how tied up you get with your work," Dorothy added, "so don't go forgetting we've got a celebration next weekend."

"A celebration?" Cammie racked her brain, the one that hadn't spit out a coherent thought in two days, trying to remember.

"Why, Cammie," her mother exclaimed, "it's *your* day. Seventeen years ago you came to live with us. You know we wouldn't miss celebrating that any more than we would Christmas."

"And this year we've got a special surprise." Edward's eyes twinkled.

"Now don't you go giving it away," Dorothy chided. "It's no surprise if you spill the beans."

"Give me a kiss, Dotty, and that'll shut me up."

"Oh, you!" She giggled girlishly before pecking him on the mouth.

Grant chuckled. "Still frisky after all these years."

"Speaking of frisky . . ." Dorothy looked Grant up and down with a mother's speculation. "When are you going to bring a girl home with you, son? Twenty-eight years old and still sowing your oats. It's a crying shame the way you carry on, and don't you think I don't know about it. Racing around in that hot rod and keeping your answering machine on till all hours. Aren't you ready to settle down *yet*?"

"I'm ready. I've *been* ready. It's just a matter of getting the right girl to settle down with me."

Cammie could feel his gaze lock on her. She darted a glance at Mom and Dad, and was grateful that they didn't seem to notice. Their attention was on Grant as they pursued one of their favorite topics. Cammie had heard it all before, but never had the words taken on such startling overtones.

"Well," Dorothy said, "when you meet her, you'll know."

"Yes." Grant made the affirmation quietly, but with enough impact that Cammie swung her gaze around to meet his. Their eyes locked for a suspended, meaningful moment. "Yes," he assured her, "that's something I've known for a long time."

"It's gettin' dark," Edward said, unintentionally breaking the tension. "You two had best hit the road before Mom lectures you into old age. Though I dare say at the rate you two young 'uns are going, you're gonna end up stuck with each other."

"Ed, what a horrible thing to say. And you think *I'm* bad about lecturing."

Edward laughed. Dorothy joined him. Grant sent Cammie a half-smile, but the force of his gaze was enough to send her reeling.

Cammie could feel herself visibly pale, while her stomach churned in a good imitation of his hot tub.

"Love you, Mom. You too, Dad." Grant gave them a parting embrace, then walked to the passenger side of the Porsche and opened the door. "Cammie, ready?"

Cammie stifled a gasp of disbelief that he would be so blatant in front of them, but was saved by Dorothy's misguided praise.

"Isn't that nice to see Grant open the door for his sister, Ed? Seems all those years we spent drilling them on manners really did sink in."

Making her final good-byes as hastily as possible, Cammie slid onto the seat. She reached for her seat belt, but Grant beat her to it.

"Let me," he whispered, for only her ears to hear.

She sat still as stone, an aura seeming to surround the spot on her hand he'd just brushed. Though he was mercifully quick, it seemed she sat there an eternity while he fastened the seat belt as their parents chatted gaily on.

Didn't they know what was happening? she wondered. Couldn't they tell she was betraying their trust? Wasn't her flushed face and thundering heartbeat enough to announce her crime, her impure response to their son? Or maybe they were as blind as she had apparently been all these years. Lucky them. Ignorance, in this case, *was* bliss.

Grant's door shut, the sound snapping her out of the mire of her thoughts. Forcing a smile, she blew a kiss to her adoptive parents as they held hands, waving good-bye.

Cammie watched them in the side-view mirror as Grant pulled away from the curb. They stood in front of the modest but cozy house they had taken her into and had insisted she belonged in as much as their own children. Her insides twisted with the memory. Was this how she paid them back for their kindness? And what about Grant? How could he so callously dismiss their feelings?

His hand reached for hers. The turmoil she felt was horrible, knowing they could possibly be creating a catastrophe. But his touch felt so incredibly right, so perfect and sure and deliciously heady.

Despite this clash of opposing forces, she didn't try to move away. It was wrong, yet too good to deny. The least she could do was punish herself with it.

She did. She didn't let herself look at Grant, but faced the mirror until home and family were mere specks in the distance.

Four

If Cammie was thankful for one thing, it was for Grant remaining silent as the miles slipped by. The only sound was the slight stream of air whistling through the window she'd cracked open, mingling with the tape pulsing out a medley of sensual songs.

Why was it, she wondered, when they had listened to the same songs so often she'd lost count, the music had never had this effect on her before? Stirring her senses, making her acutely aware of the man who so artfully stroked her palm before bringing her hand to his lips without looking away from the road.

She didn't pull free. Lord help her for being weak in a way she'd never dreamed possible. Then again, she didn't return his caresses. She forced herself not to participate, only to allow, to take.

Didn't that make her less a conspirator? Not a victim, not by a long shot, but at least not a willing participant. At least that's what she told herself, trying to ease a small measure of the guilt for enjoying it so much. Enjoy? Now that was so huge an understatement, she couldn't even swallow it herself. She was greedy for it, soaking up the wonder, the sinful richness she could easily grow to crave.

All too soon the stolen moments of their uneasy peace purred to a halt as the tires contacted the worn bricks of her driveway. Grant cut the engine, and the motor's rumble ceased. So did the music, leaving only the sound of her own breathing, too loud and erratic.

She looked straight ahead, afraid to confront whatever she might see in his dark, somber, and newly compelling gaze. Then he placed her hand on his thigh and pressed.

Cammie swallowed hard. His jeans were smooth and faded and hugged his skin tight. She felt the heat of his body through the denim, and the well-honed muscle tauten in response to her touch.

"Why?"

His whisper filled up the small space while the simple question curled disconcertingly around and through her head.

"Why . . . what?" she asked.

"*Why*, after all this time? *Why* did it take you so long? And *why* now?"

"I don't know what you mean."

The futile lie sounded hollow, even to her. She was certain Grant heard it. Damn, why did they have to know each other so well? Their closeness was fast becoming more enemy than ally.

"You know exactly what I mean," he said. "Don't try playing games with me, Cammie. You know as well as I do what's going on. I want an answer. I want to know what happened to make the change."

What happened? Oh, nothing, brother dear. I just saw you naked, and like a peeping Tom I couldn't pry my eyes away, any more than I could stop an arousal I couldn't control, that left me so weak my legs were shaking.

She took one last forbidden taste of the feel of his thigh beneath her palm, then forced her hand away. She clasped her hands tight in her lap, not trusting her wayward need.

"I . . . Grant, I don't know. All I do know is we're playing with something dangerous, and we've got to quit before it goes any further."

He ignored her warning and clasped her shoulders, forcing her to face him. She made herself try to shrug him away. He merely increased the pressure of his grip.

"You're lying, Cammie. But whatever happened, you can keep it to yourself for now. I'll gladly take the results, whatever the cause."

"It's wrong, Grant. Try all you like to deny it, what we're doing is *wrong*."

"Is it?" He lifted one hand to her neck, sliding it down the slender column with a feather-light touch, then stroking his thumb over the hollow where her pulse thrummed in a giveaway rush.

Cammie cursed herself for the immediacy of her response, for the wildness surging against her will.

"You shouldn't do that," she said.

"Yes, I should." He bent his head closer, and for a heart-stopping moment she thought he was going to kiss her. He stopped scant inches away and whispered, "How can anything so good be wrong?"

She didn't have an answer. She couldn't even think. Her throat constricted and she tried to swallow past the thickness.

"Have I ever told you what it does to me whenever our eyes meet?" he murmured.

She managed a jerky shake of her head.

Grant moved his hand up her arm and into her hair, toying with the curls at her nape.

"No? Then did I ever tell you how I wish I could bury my face in your hair?"

"No," she whispered.

He slid his fingers back up her throat to trace her bottom lip with his thumb.

"I guess you have no idea then of how many times I've imagined tasting your mouth. Not only tasting. Devouring. Kissing you, discovering how your tongue would feel, sliding against and around mine, until you slipped it into my mouth and whimpered for more."

As he spoke in a low, soothing voice, she could feel her tongue moving against her teeth, as though it begged for the freedom to indulge in his fantasy. Her breasts felt fuller, heavy and straining. She tried to deny the moistness flowing in betrayal between her thighs, but the ache was too strong to ignore the throb, the pulse.

"Please . . ." she begged. Though for what she begged, she didn't know. Was it for his illicit touch? Or was it for him to stop the insanity of this sensual, silken web he spun before she lost her slender control? She was too close to weakening, that much she knew. Shouting down her instincts, she commanded her vocal chords to form the words, "Please, Grant. Stop now."

"If that's what you really want. I won't force you into anything you don't want, Cammie. But you are fighting yourself, not me. Like it or not, you *do* want me. And we both know it."

She didn't waste her breath trying to deny it, but looked away. Grant traced her lips once more, brushed a strand of hair away from her face, then moved back until he leaned against his door.

The absence of his touch told her even more than his skillful, persuasive strokes. It left her hungering and feeling strangely empty and alone.

"I'm sorry to upset you, Cammie. I hate to see you unhappy, and I hate even more being the cause. Talk to me. Tell me what you're feeling."

Her gaze darted to his and she saw a semblance of the old comfort he had always offered. But it wasn't the same. It was . . . more.

"If I tell you what I'm feeling," she said, "doesn't that seem a bit like leaving the window open for the thief to sneak in?"

"You think I'm trying to take something away from what we've had in the past, don't you?"

"It's not the same with us, Grant, and I—I hate that."

"You're right. It's not the same. But that doesn't mean we have to lose anything. We can keep what we have. Just because we add to it, doesn't mean we have to take away."

Why did he always have to make such sense? she wondered. She'd never liked fighting with Grant because he had a way of making his point of view sound perfectly reasonable, no matter how off-base he was.

"I don't think it's that simple," she countered. "There's a price tag attached to everything in life. You never get something for free."

"True, but whatever the price might be, I'd pay it ten times over to have a life with you."

Frantically, she tried to deflect his quiet but firm, heartfelt words. They were words that could weaken her, their simplicity striking hard at her resolve.

"There's a problem, Grant, a very big problem

that you're overlooking. It wouldn't just be your price or my price to pay. Innocent people who deserve better from us could end up hurt—badly hurt."

"That's possible. Then again, you could be underestimating Mom and Dad. There's only one way to find out, and even if the worst happened and they were hurt, what's the worse crime—them having to get over a blind spot in their principles and learning to live with a situation they can't condone, or us having a whole lifetime of regret and bitterness for turning our backs on the best thing either of us could ever have?"

"Don't you think you're taking a lot for granted? Just yesterday morning you were what you've always been, and tonight you're talking changes that can affect a lot of people for their whole lives. You're going too fast, Grant."

"Maybe. But then again, I've never been what you thought I was, and the changes I'm talking about have been on my mind a long time. I've thought these same questions through till I've turned them inside out."

"Well, I haven't."

"Then I think it's time that you did."

What comfort she'd sensed earlier was gone. Grant's eyes met hers in challenge, in demand. She shifted uneasily and glanced away. He always made sense, and maybe that was why she'd always sought his counsel. Only this was different and far riskier, the stakes so high it made her queasy.

She needed time. Even more, she needed distance. She couldn't trust her judgment with her senses and emotions in such turmoil. The smartest thing she could do would be to end this conversation before it went any further.

"I think I'd better go in. It's late."

"If you say so. But we're not through talking, Cammie. Sleep on it. Think about it. And while you're at it, think about *this*."

Her breath caught sharply when in one smooth, lightning motion, he shifted her across the car and onto his lap. Her bottom was pressed against the strain of his groin, and she thought she might die of the urgency of her answering want. Before she could try to stanch her instincts, he wrapped strong arms around her, pulling her close, tucking her head into the crook of his neck while pressing her right breast against his chest.

It was the scent she had longed to inhale just this close, and she fought not to press her lips against his throat, not to thread her fingers through his hair and bring his mouth to hers. The best she could seem to do was nuzzle into his neck, keeping herself from giving in to an action she couldn't take back.

"Oh, Lord," he groaned. "It's killing me, Cammie. I've been dying by inches wanting you so much for so long; I can't ever remember not wanting you. Say you want me too."

"No," she whispered, trying desperately, futilely, to run from the truth.

He pushed his hips upward, against her. A sob of frustration caught in the back of her throat. She clutched at his shoulders as her body betrayed her and moved in counterpoint, seeking to soothe the unbearable ache.

She heard the vibration, felt it against her lips, as he moaned in response. His breath rushed hot against her hair as he worked his mouth into the thickness and brought a hand up to stroke the mass of curls.

Her scalp tingled while her heart hammered against his chest. She could feel the rapid beat of his heart answering hers, and she pressed closer until they meshed, until she didn't know which was his and which was hers because they seemed to beat as one.

At first, the caress was so light, she didn't realize it was he causing the rise of her nipple, not until he increased the pressure to a rhythmic, insistent thrum.

Then he was freely stroking her breast until she thought she might go mad with the delicious pleasure. She didn't cry out from the near hurt of her straining nipples, but he was only making the throb between her thighs worse by moving against her, retreating, and arching up again. And she was grinding herself against him, because she couldn't help herself if her life depended upon it.

His hand stroked slow and deliberate over her knee, then up, up, between her thighs. Silently she cursed the jeans she wore for muting his already scalding touch. When she should have been closing tight her knees, she gave in to the never-before experience of allowing her senses full rein.

Then he pressed his palm over her mound and curled his fingers into her still-shielded heat.

"Grant," she sobbed. "Grant."

"It's not enough. Sweet heaven, I've waited so long, it's just not enough."

Suddenly she felt him leave her and she wanted to weep for the loss, but then there was the press of his fingers releasing the button, and the hiss of her zipper as he rapidly slid it down.

What was she doing? she wondered frantically. What was she letting him do? Oh, Lord, Lord, she couldn't be letting this happen. But she was, she was someone else, someone she'd never been before, pleading for the crime, for the release, and not caring about tomorrow or who might be hurt in the process.

"No," she whimpered suddenly. "No, don't . . ."

"Yes. Oh, God, *yes* . . ."

And he did. He pushed past the lace of her panties, groaning as he touched the forbidden texture of her hidden curls. Then he slid his fingers between the folds of her flesh and the cloth of her pants.

Her breath hissed between her clenched teeth, and she cried out at the overwhelming sensation. If she died now, she knew it would be worth it just to embrace this taste of ecstasy at long last.

His fingers slid back and forth against her wetness, and she knew in that instant that if he breached the barrier, she would beg him to make love to her. She was mad with wanting him. Just as she had to be mad to allow what was happening, because she was so far gone, if they didn't stop now there would be no stopping.

"Cammie . . . *Cammie* . . . touch *me* . . . "

Outwardly, she was shivering. Internally, she was contracting and grasping only emptiness, and the one man who could fill her was a man she had no right to have. But how would he feel in her hand . . . inside her body . . . She ached for the knowledge.

Her hand drifted down from his chest, and he shifted, parting his legs farther, giving her access.

She stopped.

"I can't." Her chest heaved with a sob she contained. "Forgive me, Grant. I *can't*. And . . . oh, God, what are we doing?"

"More than just *this*." His finger grazed over her in a slow, erotic, and loving caress. "So much more than this, Cammie. Enough that there's nothing to forgive if you can't touch me. I can wait. You shared yourself and I love you for that, for more reasons than I could ever name."

When she would have given in to the melting, in to the sensation of him anchored in the harbor of her heart, he squeezed her once before gently letting her go, tugging the zipper back up and refastening her jeans. He embraced her and held her so close, she thought her skin would become his.

"I'd better see you inside before I lose a grip on my good intentions," he whispered into her ear.

"You're a very special man, Grant."

She rubbed her cheek against his, loving the feel of his late-night beard abrading her soft skin.

"I'm glad you think so. But I'm also very human. *Too* human when it comes to you."

His voice held an undercurrent of warning she couldn't mistake, and she quickly drew away. His eyes met hers, and even in the shadows she saw just how human he really was. The fire of unappeased hunger washed over her, almost staggering in its intensity.

Without another word, he opened the car door and drew her out with him. She reached for her purse while he unlatched the small trunk to retrieve her dress and a bag of leftovers Dorothy had sent along.

At the front door, she fumbled awkwardly with her keys, afraid he would try to kiss her—a fear that seemed pretty ridiculous after what had just transpired.

"I'll get it." He already had his own key in the lock. He opened the door, and she thought for the first time that their having keys to each other's houses was not a good idea in light of the intimacy they had shared.

As if reading her thoughts, Grant flipped on the

porch light and held his set of keys between them, the yellow glow glinting off the metal. His eyes meeting hers in challenge, he slowly returned the keys to his pocket.

Want to make an issue of it, Cammie? his gaze silently asked. *You'll have to dig for it if you want it back, and I wouldn't advise that at the moment.*

"Wait here," he said when she didn't move or speak. "I'll go check out the house to make sure you're safe."

"Really, Grant, you don't have to—"

"Wait here."

She watched his retreating back as he strode down the front hall of her quaint, old-fashioned home, flipping lights on, then off again. His shoulders had always been broad, but now they seemed far broader. And his walk had always been something she liked about Grant, but now she saw it as even more assured, as though he could forge a trail where no one else could see past the wilderness.

She dropped her purse beside the couch where Grant had left her dress and the paper sack filled with food. The scent of home cooking wafted through the room. She couldn't smell the aroma without thinking of Mom stirring something at the stove while she hummed, or looking up from the oven, her face flushed from the heat, and, after letting them lick the bowl of batter, setting out a plate of hot chocolate chip cookies and telling her and Grant that it was their job to sample them.

Cammie stared at the bag, the memories creeping insidiously through her mind to rob her of the wrongful joy she had so weakly succumbed to.

She couldn't take it back. And it was too wonderful to want to, the womanly part of her nature cherishing an experience that had made her feel more than human, and yet the most human she had ever been.

Only it was tainted now by reality, the staggering repercussions that could reach far beyond the present.

"All's clear."

She jumped at the sound of his voice, then again as he rested his hands on her shoulders and turned her around to face him. Cammie cursed herself for being a coward, but she couldn't make herself meet his gaze, especially when the unsated remnants of desire still lapped at her.

"What's wrong?" he asked.

"I feel guilty."

He muttered a low, graphic curse.

"Don't be angry with me, Grant."

He tilted her face up until she looked at him. She read frustration in his eyes, but understanding as well.

"I don't want you to feel guilty," he said, "and I can't help but resent it that you do. But what's making me angry more than anything are the circumstances we can't control."

She nodded, feeling the sting of unwanted tears. Too much had happened, and she couldn't lay the blame at Grant's feet. She had been a willing participant, after all; she and Grant had been partners in crime. It was horrible to feel so wonderful about giving in to the forbidden.

"Grant, I'm so confused. And I'm scared."

"Don't be. I'm here."

"That's what scares me."

"Ah, Cammie, don't be afraid of me. We've always been there for each other."

"Be there for me now?" She could feel the salty sting break loose as she whispered, "Hold me, Grant. Hold me like you used to."

"I don't know if I can do that, Cammie." He drew her into his arms and cradled her head against his chest. "Because I want to hold you even better."

She didn't try to stop them. She let the tears fall, the confusion spilling out from inside her. Grant rocked her back and forth, giving her comfort while he threaded his fingers through her hair.

When she was spent, she let him support her, leaning into the strength he offered. It was then she realized that while he had soothed her, something else had happened as well.

His hand was cupping her buttocks and he was hard, his erection pressing into the softness of her belly. She looked up at him, and his eyes simmered with an odd mixture of tenderness and riveting hunger.

"I can't stop what you do to me," he said softly, "and I'll never apologize for wanting you so bad, it's eating me alive. But I care enough to give you what you need before taking what I want."

He lowered his head, and she prayed he wouldn't try to kiss her. She could feel the momentum of passion gather, wanting it as much as he did, and that want was as unwelcome as it was strong.

He pressed his lips against her forehead, and she shut her eyes in gratitude and weariness and disappointment. Before he could work his way down, she latched onto what surely was as wise as it was painfully difficult to say.

"I . . . need some time alone, Grant."

"I know."

"Don't call me or come see me this week . . . please."

His hands tensed. "If that's what you want."

She didn't want it, any more than she wanted him to leave. But it was rational, her only hope to make some sense of this insanity that was unraveling their lives.

"It's . . . yes. It *is* what I want."

"Then I'll pick you up Saturday morning. We can talk on the way to Mom and Dad's."

The celebration, of course. She dreaded it already. How could she face them after tonight? How could she sit next to Grant in their driveway in the very car they had nearly made love in?

"I—" She took a deep breath, steeling herself. "I think it would be a good idea if we took separate cars."

"Son of a—Dammit, I know what you're thinking and I want you to quit it." His voice was harsh. "Quit wallowing in your guilt, Cammie Walker. I won't have it."

He gripped her arms tight, and his brows drew together ominously as his mouth loomed dangerously close to hers.

"No, Grant." She shook her head in fierce denial, as much for her own benefit as his. "Don't do it."

"Don't worry," he growled. "When I kiss you it won't be with any reservations on your part. As much as I'd love to ravage your mouth right now and drive out that conscience that's working overtime, you'd regret it the minute I was out the door."

He released her abruptly, uttering a curse.

She watched him stalk to the door, frustration and anger evident in each step.

"Grant, wait. Listen—"

"No, *you* listen." He swung around and pointed a stern finger at her. "While you're thinking it all over this week, keep one thing in mind. What we could have together is something a lot of people don't find in an entire lifetime. The guilt that's all over your face is going to poison what could be honorable and good between us. Think hard,

Cammie. Because what I want with you has no room for guilt."

She stared after him as he shut the door firmly behind him. Almost immediately he opened it again and reached in to flip the latch.

His face was still thunderous as he ordered, "Don't forget the chain."

Slumping onto the couch, she nearly sat on the paper sack reminder. She hurled the bag across the room, then buried her face into an old pillow she had made when Mom had taught her to cross-stitch.

"Damn it all to hell," she cried, pounding the cushions.

Raising her head, she stared at the door he had locked, and felt the familiar sense of protection Grant had always provided. She also felt the unfamiliar ache between her thighs he had created and left unsatisfied.

How was she *not* supposed to feel guilty about that? For once Grant hadn't been understanding when she really needed it. He was different as a man, and even alone now she flushed to remember the intimacy he had initiated while she had been so shamelessly eager to succumb.

Sweet Lord, they had almost made love. She had only herself to blame for letting it get out of control. But hadn't Grant loved her enough to stop when she had asked?

Love. Why did there have to be so many kinds and why did one have to be sacrificed for another? Or choices made of whom you loved more loyally?

The questions gave birth to so many others, she finally shut them all out. Emotionally drained, she wrung what few tears she had left onto the couch.

It held no warmth or comfort. It held no heat, no flesh and blood reminder that there was a man who loved her and had the power to make her body weep.

Five

The problem with safe but outdated cars, Cammie decided, was that in their old age they had a propensity for failing health. She grimaced as the oil light flashed on. Thank goodness she was only a few miles away from Mom and Dad's. She had some extra oil with her, but come Monday she was going to have a transportation problem.

Grant had always been there to help her out before, glad to give her a lift about town. She would have to find another alternative this time.

Her stomach lurched at the thought of him. It had been lurching for the last five and a half days. She wondered if she was working on an ulcer.

Food was tasteless. She couldn't sleep. She couldn't think straight, even with his all-too-blatant absence. She missed him like crazy, and misery was her only company.

As it must continue to be. She still couldn't come to terms with what they had done, any more than she could accept the responsibility for possibly creating a rift in the family.

The question she had pondered about Grant's attitude toward his parents' ability or inability to deal with the situation had at least come into focus. He belonged to the family by birth, and therefore felt he had the right to call his own shots.

She, on the other hand, had been taken in because of their generosity. Because of that, she felt compelled to earn her right to belong, to prove she was worthy of their unconditional love.

As she rounded a last familiar curve, the white wood house gleamed in the sun, the bright red shutters winking in welcome. She had always found comfort in coming home, but not today. Grant's car was parked out front.

The twist in her stomach was joined by a tightening in her lungs. An ominous and disturbing sense of premonition shot through her fragile resolve to stay calm.

Pulling behind his car, Cammie frantically wondered how in heaven's name she was going to pull this off. She was frankly terrified to see him again—terrified and hopelessly eager, because she had never missed anyone in her life the way she had missed Grant that week.

Shamefully, she had to admit she had been craving the newfound sensations he created as well. Even a touch of his hand or a secret message in her eyes would be heaven.

She cursed when the chrome door handle slipped in her grip, her hands were sweating so bad. No sooner had her feet touched the ground than Trish rushed out the front door.

"Cammie! My favorite sister!"

Cammie found herself wrapped in Trish's usual enthusiastic greeting. Her vivacious personality was reflected in her bright purple, red, and yellow sundress. She wore it with more a model's ease than that of a young widow who taught home ec. With her long dark hair and wholesome good looks, Trish could have passed for Grant's twin instead of his older sister. But since she and Cammie shared the same birthday, the family always said *they* were the twins—just long lost, since Cammie was delivered late.

"What do you mean, your *favorite* sister?" Cammie said. "I'm your *only* sister!" Hard as it was, she managed the lighthearted comeback she always gave in their little ritual.

"Let me look at you," Trish said, holding Cammie at arm's length. Looking her up and down, Trish shook her head with a small look of disapproval. "What in tarnation has happened to make you lose so much weight? You look ten pounds lighter than the last time I saw you. Ten pounds in two months? Must be man trouble."

Oh, Lord! Cammie thought. If she only knew.

"Make it more like six pounds," she said. "But at least I can fit back into that skirt that was getting too tight." She didn't add it had only taken one week to lose the weight. "And it's more like work trouble than man trouble." Liar, liar, pants on fire, her conscience taunted.

"Problems on the job?" Trish asked.

"Not exactly. Just a lot of stress and long hours. Goes with the position."

"Hmmm." Trish gave her an "if you say so" look. "We'll talk later, after you've had a chance to be mobbed by the natives."

"Where's Audrey?" Cammie asked, not willing to commit to a heart-to-heart. "Usually she's the first one out the door to tackle me."

"She's with Grant. He finished that project he's been working on. You know, Audrey's Fine Line. At least, that's what he's dubbed it. He promised

Audrey that if he sold the design, he'd make sure it was part of the deal that her name was on the packaging. That man . . ."

Trish's doe-brown eyes sparkled with pride and deep affection. "I don't know what we'd do without him. Ever since I lost Mark, he's been the closest thing to a father figure Audrey could have. I tell you, whoever lands him is going to be one lucky lady. Too bad he's our brother, huh, Cammie?"

"Umm . . . yeah. Too bad."

Cammie shifted uncomfortably. Her answer had come out strained and unintentionally abrupt. She hadn't even gone into the house yet, and she already felt like Chinese water torture would be a pleasure compared to this.

"Guess we'd better go in," Cammie said brightly. Her insides twisted as Trish's brow wrinkled in puzzlement at her odd behavior. "Otherwise, they'll come looking for us."

She hooked her arm through Trish's and headed them toward the house, filling the strange gap in their conversation with some overly animated chatter. Cammie could hear the higher pitch of her own voice, the nervous agitation goading her on when she would have given anything to run back to her car and escape to the blessed silence of her home.

"Look what the cat dragged in, everybody!" Trish shouted as soon as they neared the kitchen, where the bustle of activity and delicious smells mingled in familiar welcome.

Cammie's heart was running so fast and her lungs were squeezing so tight, she prayed she didn't pass out before she could paste on a fake smile and an equally fake attitude of exuberance.

"The Guest of Honor has officially arrived," Edward's voice boomed above the mayhem.

"Surprise!"
"Surprise!"
"Surprise!"

The cacophony of the Kennedy clan and Dorothy's assorted relations reverberated against the pounding rush of the panic that threatened to engulf her. Dorothy was the first in line, embracing her with the smell of freshly baked bread, brisket, pecan pie, and . . . home.

"Cammie, sweetheart. Happy adoption day." She dabbed at her eyes and kissed Cammie on either cheek. "Are you surprised? We decided to invite everyone this year, instead of just the immediate family. It really took some doing to park the cars out of sight, though I imagine you heard the ruckus clear to Austin. Oh, and Aunt Frieda sends her love. She was the only one who couldn't make it. Poor dear, she broke her hip last week. But she sent you a big jar of her blue-ribbon picante sauce!"

"Aunt Frieda's picante sauce," Cammie managed to exclaim enthusiastically. "Now *that's* a real treat. And here I thought I had to wait till Christmas." While she spoke, her eyes darted around for a glimpse of Grant. She didn't see him, and strangely her heart sank at the same time she breathed a sigh of relief.

"Looking for Grant, honey?" Cammie's gaze shot back to Dorothy, who was already being nudged aside by Aunt Mabel, her presence announced by her trademark scent—a too generous splash of White Shoulders. "He's in the other room with Audrey," Dorothy went on. "He wanted me to tell you to come keep them company if you waded through here before dinnertime. And, oh my, it must be too warm in here. Your cheeks are so flushed, sweetheart."

"Just the excitement, Mom," she quickly hedged, praying anxiety and misery and guilt weren't written all over her face. "You and Dad really surprised me this time."

For the next hour she endured hefty bosom hugs, teary eyes, too many kisses to count, too many ailment recountings to list, and enough pats on the back to last a lifetime. In the past, it would have been a high point of the year, an assurance that she was indeed loved and accepted. But now, she felt claustrophobic, all but smothered by the family reunion held in her honor.

After the eternity of greetings subsided, she excused herself to the bathroom. Once in the white-tiled haven of antiquated fixtures, she locked the door and slumped against it. Drawing several deep breaths, she commanded herself to relax, to quit shaking, and for heaven's sake *not* to have a panic attack.

She was splashing cold water over her face when a soft knock sounded at the door. Cammie tensed. Was it Grant hunting her down?

"Yes?" she called breathlessly.

"It's me, Trish. Can I come in?"

Cammie stared at the mirror and was distressed to see her facade had disappeared, revealing the true rawness of her emotional state. Quickly trying to readjust her features into a suitable mask, she turned off the water and opened the door.

Trish slipped quickly in, then locked the door behind her.

"Too much, huh?" she asked sympathetically.

Cammie let the mask slip a notch. "Too much," she confirmed.

"Mind if I smoke?"

"What? *You* smoke? When did you pick up that nasty habit?"

"Not long after Mark died. Stupid, I know. But I do it anyway." She opened the window, then fished a lighter and pack of cigarettes out of a side pocket on her dress. "Mom and Dad don't know, of course." She turned and smiled conspiratorially. "You won't tell on me, will you?"

"Of course not. We always had a pact to cover for each other if it looked like trouble. Remember?"

"I remember. I just wanted to make sure *you* did." Lighting up, Trish carefully directed the smoke out the window before turning a knowing gaze on Cammie. "What's wrong, Sis?"

Cammie looked away. Damn, she thought. Why was everything she'd counted a blessing turning out to be a curse? Trish never missed a trick, and they had always confided their darkest secrets to each other.

But none this dark.

"There is something wrong," she admitted slowly. "But it's something I've got to work out myself, Trish. I—I just can't talk about it." She gave her a weak smile. "But thanks for asking anyway. You're not just a good sister, you're an even better friend."

Trish considered her as she took another puff. "That bad, Cammie?"

"That bad."

"Well, you know I'm always on your side. No matter what."

"Same here. And Trish . . . if I talked to anyone about . . . the problem, it would be you."

"Not Grant?"

Trish eyed her shrewdly, waiting while she fanned the smoke outside.

Cammie took a deep breath, hoping her usually transparent face didn't betray her.

"Guess we'd better get back before they send a

search party." Some answer, she thought, but it was the best she could do. Lying wasn't her forte, and that last question she wouldn't touch with a ten-foot pole.

"Good idea." Trish smiled in a very strange, pleased sort of way, as though she'd gotten the answer she was looking for. "Let me get rid of the evidence first. Can't have Mom and Dad thinking we're less than perfect."

"Trish!" Cammie gasped in genuine astonishment. "It's not like you to say something like that."

"No," she agreed, dumping the smoldering cigarette butt into the commode, along with the ashes she'd flicked into her hand. "But I think it a lot. Sometimes I get tired of living up to the image— you know, the perfect, all-American family. Mom and Dad and apple pie. If they weren't so great, it'd be a lot easier on us. I mean, then we wouldn't have to always worry about letting them down or hurting their feelings."

"I . . . actually, I never thought about it that way, Trish. They've done so much for me, I only know I'd hate myself if I ever brought them grief."

"Yeah, me too. Guess that's why I'm a thirty-one-year-old woman sneaking cigarettes in the bathroom and swishing mouthwash so they don't smell it on my breath."

Trish gargled for emphasis, then spat the mouthwash into the sink.

Cammie laughed for the first time in what seemed ages. What Trish had said made her feel better. Whether Trish suspected the truth about Grant, she didn't know for certain, but at least she was reassured that Trish would understand the ordeal she was going through.

Cammie reached for the doorknob, her flagging

spirits buoyed. With a giggle reminiscent of days gone by, she turned to Trish.

"I wonder how many bottles of White Shoulders Aunt Mabel goes through a year?"

Trish wrinkled her nose and fanned the air. "I don't know, but at least enough to compete with Aunt Frieda's basementful of blue-ribbon picante sauce."

They rolled their eyes and groaned in unison, before dissolving into a much-needed fit of laughter.

When they caught their breath, Cammie impulsively reached for Trish's hand and squeezed it.

"That was good, Trish. I needed it more than you could know."

"I needed it too. Hey, tell you what, Cammie. Since you covered for me stealing a smoke, why don't I return the favor?"

"You'll be the Guest of Honor?"

Trish snickered. "Don't push it. But I will do my best to get the ritual sing-along going, so you can disappear for a while without too much fuss. Uncle Harold's been after me to play the piano all morning so he can do his rendition of 'The Yellow Rose of Texas.'"

"If only he weren't so hard-of-hearing, maybe he'd know how off-key he is."

Trish reached into her pocket and pulled out a pair of earplugs. "I came prepared this year. It's murder trying not to laugh. Now scram before you miss your chance."

"I owe you, Trish. Thanks for buying me some time."

"Sure." They stepped out into the hall, and Trish cocked her head in the direction of the "study room" where they used to do their homework. "Grant's in there."

Before Cammie could manage more than an unintelligible stutter, Trish was already in the overcrowded living room and announcing that the sing-along was about to begin.

Did she know? Cammie wondered. Surely Grant hadn't told her. So why . . . how?

The heavy steps behind her sounded suspiciously like they belonged to Aunt Mabel. Quickly ducking into the foyer leading to the study room, Cammie didn't give herself time to weigh the wisdom of her decision.

She would just steal a glance, she told herself. What could it hurt to look at him, if that was all she did? The longing had been building since the minute he'd left her home a week ago, and now she was starved for just the sight of him . . . the feel of him, the magic of his touch—*No*. She *had* to stop thinking like that. The only way she could allow herself to look was if she vowed not to give in to the forbidden.

Slowly twisting the knob, she quietly pushed the door inward. He was talking to Audrey, and his voice washed over her, evoking a fresh wave of longing, of all the indecent memories she had basked in, despite her stern resolve not to.

She slipped into the room unnoticed, then pressed the door shut and simply watched.

It was a cozy, cluttered room, a little dark without windows, illuminated only by the fluorescent light shining into the fifty-gallon aquarium along the far wall.

Grant had his back to her, but she could see Audrey perched on his knees, chattering on excitedly about the "fishy" she had just caught.

Cammie's gaze roved over him hungrily. She remembered all too well how it felt to sit on his lap. She remembered the feel of his muscles as she had held onto the shoulders she craved to run her hands over now.

"Okay, Audrey," he said, "now here's the tricky part. We don't want to hurt the fish, or scare him too much, since we want to play this game again."

"Again and again, Uncle Grant. And I know how to let him go nice. See? Just like this." The sound of a switch clicking brought a gurgle of laughter from the small five-year-old girl.

"Very good, Audrey."

"I did it right!"

"You did it perfect. Look at him swim away now. After they get used to this and know you'll let them out of the net, maybe the fish will decide they like the game too."

"I want to do it again, Uncle Grant."

"Okay, and this time you can try it all by yourself."

Cammie watched as Grant released Audrey's small hands to work the simple controls of the two-foot-long rod and reel—minus the hook. A pulley worked by a flip switch either expanded or contracted the opening of the net, which "caught" the goldfish without the need for bait.

"I did it! I did it!" Audrey squealed in delight.

"You most certainly did, young lady. I think you must be the best fisherman I ever met under four feet tall."

"Wow, and that's a lot."

Grant's deep chuckle brought a smile to Cammie's lips. Trish was right. He'd always been wonderful with Audrey, trying to fill her father's shoes the best he could. He had a natural knack with kids. Not that he didn't lose his patience sometimes, but he genuinely liked them, and they always seemed to gravitate in his direction.

She had known that, and yet she had never

quite seen him in this light. Today he seemed more paternal, the kind of man any child would be blessed to have as a father. She could just envision him giving a toddler a piggyback ride, wrestling with a couple of kids on the floor, coaching Little League, or even changing a diap—

What in the world was she thinking about? She knew she should get the hell out of there before she asked him to be a sperm donor—minus the doctor's assistance.

"Going somewhere, Cammie?"

Her hand froze as she reached for the knob, his voice seeming to drift temptingly down to her heart. She felt as though something languorous and dizzy and sweet had just replaced the blood in her veins.

"I was afraid they would miss me at the party," she said weakly.

"Not nearly as much as I'd miss you being here."

She turned, and that was her fatal mistake. Their eyes met and held, and as if he had an invisible lure of his own, he reeled her in closer . . . closer.

Six

Grant had been hoping she would come to him. He was so starved for her, a touch of her hand on his arm would be sheer delight. He clamped down the impulse to rush to her, crush her to him, and reassure himself that last week's miracle was actually real.

With infinitely more patience than he was feeling, he lifted Audrey as he stood, then carefully set the girl back down on the stool. She was so absorbed in her new toy, she simply grinned and flipped the latch to release her newest catch.

"Hi, Aunt Cammie," she said while skimming the line through the water. "Watch me get the guppy this time."

"I'm watching," Cammie assured her in a breathy voice that wasn't lost on Grant. "He's a big one, Audrey. A real trophy winner."

"Maybe we should have him mounted," Grant suggested, forcing himself to keep it light when all he wanted to do was back her into the wall and take the kiss that was way past due. The one he'd been kicking himself all week for not taking, in spite of her maddening refusal.

They stood close, Audrey suddenly forgotten. Grant couldn't look away from her face any more than he could stanch the immediate surge of desire, culminating in a familiar pain around his heart and radiating down to his groin. Her pupils dilated. He could feel the hum of mutual need and remembrance, so strong and electric it was a wonder it didn't roll off them, connect with the water, and shock them both.

"This has been about the longest week of my life," he murmured, low and intimate. "I've missed you like hell, Cammie."

"I've . . . it's been a long week for me too, Grant."

He wanted more, but it brought him face-to-face with the battle he knew lay ahead. His strategy was plotted, and he wasn't wasting a minute assaulting her defenses.

"Long enough to think about what happened . . . and what didn't?"

"Long enough to realize—" she glanced away, then back, as though she was too hungry for the sight of him to deny herself that much. "To realize we—*I*—should have behaved more responsibly."

"Do you regret it?"

"No. But that doesn't make it right."

"Not being true to yourself isn't right. Hiding from your feelings isn't right. They catch up to you sooner or later, Cammie. Avoiding the inevitable is a fool's game."

"Just as fooling around is a very *dangerous* game."

"Who's fooling around? This is serious business and you know it as well as I do."

Because he couldn't stand the abstinence another second, because he couldn't forget how her hair had wrapped around his hands like silken chains, binding him irrevocably to the only woman he could ever love . . . and just because he wanted to, he stroked his hand over her flushed cheek and into her thick hair.

Her response was immediate—the heady catch of her breath, the smoky turbulence in her gaze, which obliterated the caution he would stop at nothing to destroy.

"Uncle Grant, why are you playing with Aunt Cammie's hair?"

Damn, he thought. Cammie pulled back instantly. He gripped the nape of her neck, refusing the distance and holding her prisoner.

"I'm fixing it for the party, Audrey. Isn't it pretty?"

"Sure is. I want hair just like Aunt Cammie's. Will you fix mine too, Uncle Grant?"

"Okay, under one condition. You skedaddle so I can tell Aunt Cammie a secret."

"Ohh," Audrey moaned. "Do I have to? I wanna fish some more."

"You can. But I'll bet Uncle Brian could give you a few pointers on catching that algae eater we couldn't get off the side. Why don't you go show him your new rod and reel and find out what we should do. When you come back, we'll give it another try."

"Well . . ."

"I'll bet you a dollar you can't do it."

"A whole dollar?" Audrey promptly reeled in her line and hopped off the stool. "Oh boy! I'd be rich!"

The second she was out the door, Cammie whirled on him. "You bribed her, Grant."

"Damn right. And if the dollar hadn't worked I would have gone for a candy store. Audrey should have held out."

"She knew something wasn't right," Cammie said urgently. "Even as young as she is, she noticed. What does that tell you about how long it would be before other people started to catch on?"

"Let them." In one swift, fluid motion he reversed their places so she was right where he wanted her, with her back to the wall, a bookcase and the aquarium on either side. "If we're lucky we've got ten minutes alone. That's not much time, Cammie. Let's make the most of it."

"What are you thinking, Grant? The entire family's on the other side of the wall. Let me go."

"Not on your life. I've waited all week to get this close. Hell, I've waited forever. You can scream if you want to, but considering you want to be so secretive, I don't advise it."

"Don't you have any principles? Don't you even *care*?"

"I've got principles. Not that I need them, since you seem to have enough for us both. And yes, I *do* care. I care too much to ever let you get away." He leaned into her, forcing her to endure what he knew was an excitement she didn't want. "Quit squirming. I'm still so hard from last week I'm hurting, so do us both a favor and be still before I do something rash. All I want right now is to talk."

She went suddenly still. "Then move away. We can talk better if we're not in each others' faces."

"Why? So you can think some more while you keep me at a distance? No way." He cupped her face in both hands when she tried to roll her head away. "How can you talk about the problem when you're afraid to confront exactly what it is?"

"Okay, Grant," she said, her voice shaking. "We *do* have a problem. A very big one."

"Yes," he agreed with an ironic chuckle, "Indeed it is a *big* problem. But it goes a lot further than that. We can work better as a team than we can playing hide-and-seek. Let's quit hiding from reality, Cammie, and seek some solutions to make it work."

"I've thought, Grant, believe me. I don't see how it can work. Not without doing a great deal of damage that could possibly never be repaired. It's very selfish of us to let something as superficial as passion make decisions that can never be taken back."

His anger was swift and deep. Grant struggled to keep his voice even, struggled to keep his hands off her arms so he could shake some sense into her.

"Is that what all your thinking this week netted you? The realization that we were caught up in some temporary kind of hormonal rush?"

"I . . ." She paled. "I told myself that, yes. We've known each other so long, Grant. It's—it's insane."

"Insane? I've got news for you, lady. This is as real as it gets. Feeling you move against me was *real*, making you so hot you were melting into my hand was *real*. Hearing you moan my name while I found out you were so tight you could be a virgin—"

She suddenly thrust away from him, her face ashen. Grant pushed her back against the wall, blocking her escape.

"Stop it, Grant. I don't want to hear anymore—"

"Too bad, because you're hearing me out." He anchored her face between his hands, forging mercilessly on. "You're right, all that was passion. It was the most incredible physical desire I've ever felt in my life, though God knows it was just enough to whet my appetite. But to hear you say it was no more than that makes me sick. All my life I've been waiting—"

The door suddenly opened, the roar of voices spilling over the heat of his outrage.

"Grant? What are you and Cammie up to?"

"Hi, Mom," he said, his frustration barely contained. "I was just—"

"Helping me get an eyelash out of my eye." Cammie bolted with spring-action reflexes, rushing past him and refusing to meet his gaze. "Thanks, Grant. Much better. Mom, can I give you a hand in the kitchen? I know you've been working nonstop all morning."

"And loving every minute of it. And *no*, you may not help me on *your* day. Besides, I've already got too much help in the kitchen. Wash up, Grant, it's time to eat. I just came to call you both to dinner."

"Thanks, Mom," he muttered as the door shut behind them. "Thanks a whole hell of a lot."

Cammie wondered if the agony that was passing itself off as dinner was ever going to end. Grant's constant stare was sandwiched between Dorothy's motherly concern about where her appetite was and admonitions that she needed to put on some weight. The only relief she found was in the sympathetic squeeze Trish gave her hand under the table before she commanded everyone's attention with a vivid recounting of a scandal at school.

One grueling ordeal rolled into another. As soon as dessert was served, everyone gathered around to sing "Happy Adoption Day to You," then took turns presenting her with a gift.

"Aunt Mabel, how sweet of you. White Shoulders talc and body lotion. I can't wait to take a bath and put some on."

Without looking up, she could feel Grant's eyes boring into her. She could hear his thoughts—

the idea of smoothing it on her mingling with the anger she knew was still simmering close to the surface.

Grant was a man of purpose, and in spite of his independent thinking, his moral fiber was equally strong. She had offended him with her absurd suggestion that the power surging between them was only a physical whim. That was a crock and she knew it, but she'd been grasping at straws.

"I drew it just for you," Audrey said as Cammie opened the girl's gift. "Mommy bought me new colors. I liked the purple for your hair. Don't forget, Uncle Grant, you promised to fix mine like Aunt Cammie's."

Cammie snapped out of her trance, the crayon drawing barely registering as she hugged Audrey, not risking a glance at her parents for their reaction to the innocently spoken words.

It was needless, she realized moments later. Grant ironically proved her salvation.

"I hope you like them," he said as he handed her his gift. His fingers brushed hers, eliciting a thousand tiny thrills.

She fumbled with the small package, her hands shaking with awareness of the tension crackling between them. Awareness of him, of their audience—and of her anticipation of receiving a gift from Grant, one given with overtones that had never been there in the past.

Opening the jeweler's box, she gasped. Everyone leaned near, trying to catch a glimpse of the diamond-and-aquamarine-studded hairpins nestled into sapphire velvet. Personal . . . yet far more personal than anyone there could guess.

"They're beautiful," she breathed, even the onlookers unable to diminish her awe. "Grant, they're . . . I've looked at these every time I've passed the jeweler's window for the last two years."

"i know," he said quietly, with an undercurrent only she would recognize. "You kept me waiting enough times while you window-shopped."

She looked up at him as if in slow motion. The desire to throw her arms around his neck and kiss him sweet and hot was so strong, she yearned for life to have been different, his parents no longer hers.

As she tilted her head up, he smiled the smile of a secret lover. Then he lifted a pin out and worked it into her hair. She strongly suspected his clumsiness was feigned, an excuse to toy with her hair longer than he should, to stroke his fingers against her scalp and create tingling, rippling chills.

When both pins were in, everyone applauded—whether for the spectacular gift or Grant's seeming accomplishment, she wasn't sure.

"Ladies and gentlemen. Friends and relatives," he announced, "I propose a toast to the loveliest lady to grace our TV sets each night." Everyone raised iced-tea glasses or beer mugs. "Here's to our Cammie. She's special. And she's ours."

A cheer went up as glasses clinked and several sniffles were heard, Grant leaned down and kissed her on the cheek.

Appearances dictated a chaste kiss, and outwardly that was what they all saw. But Cammie felt his breath wisp against her ear, the tiny, hidden flick of his tongue; heard the whispered, "But most of all she's *mine*."

Her head was still spinning, the sweet lushness of the exchange humming through her veins, when Dorothy and Edward handed her their present next.

" A locket!" she exclaimed. "A gold heart. And the

diamond and aquamarine match the hairpins. Thank you, Mom and Dad. It's perfect."

"We found out what Grant had in store and decided you needed a set to wear on the news. Open it," Dorothy urged.

Cammie unlatched the catch, and a miniature family portrait glared back at her, quickly stealing the thunder of her joy.

Tears sparked her eyes.

"How silly of me," she said, impatiently brushing them away and swift to disguise the source. "I'm such a sentimental fool."

"You get that honest enough," Edward said with a chuckle while tears brimmed in Dorothy's eyes.

"Here, put it on me," Cammie said. "I'll only take it off when I have to. And I'll treasure it always."

"Turn it around so we can all see it," Uncle Brian said after Dorothy fastened the locket.

Cammie gulped down the bitter taste in her throat and opened the locket, holding it out for all the relatives to witness the perfect, loving family in the portrait.

The family she could splinter.

They took turns going on and on about how lucky they all were when the world was such a mess, and wasn't it wonderful that Edward and Dorothy had such smart, good-looking, outstanding children. Why, they were kids any parents would be proud of.

The parents in question were agreeing heartily, and all Cammie could think was that she wanted to be sick, she wanted to scream, "No! You're wrong! You're all wrong. We're not perfect. I'm weak and I'm human and if you only knew the truth you'd be appalled and half of you wouldn't want to lay eyes on me again for ruining the illusion."

She made herself scan the table, and everyone there blended into a horrible collage, until she accidentally met Grant's steely gaze.

His lips were compressed and his eyes were flat, hard. He shook his head slightly, his resentment blatantly obvious—to her. Everyone else seemed blind to it all.

"Cammie," Trish said brightly, her own expression reflecting some kind of understanding, "your vacation's in a week. What sort of plans have you got lined up?"

Cammie managed a smile of gratitude for Trish's breaking Grant's visual line of fire.

"I'm not really sure. I'd like to get away, though. Some peace and quiet is what I have in mind."

"What about Mom and Dad's getaway?" Trish suggested.

"Cammie, sweetheart, you're welcome to the cottage if you want to spend some time there." Dorothy reached across the table to squeeze Cammie's hand. "The lake's peaceful and there's not another soul around for miles. The pantry's stocked, so you wouldn't have to bother with many groceries."

Cammie thought for a moment. Two weeks alone with no work and no phone and no family? It was exactly what she needed to try to get her world back on track. She could think and get her act together, put everything into perspective. It was paramount for her to get a firm grip. She couldn't go on this way and keep her sanity.

"That sounds like a great idea," she said. "Two weeks at the cottage alone would be the perfect vacation."

"Are you sure you want to go all alone?" Dorothy asked. "What if you got hurt? You know Dad saw a big rattler last year, and if he hadn't had his boots on he could have been a goner the way that thing kept striking." Dorothy shivered. "Oh, those things scare me. And remember that drifter that came by when you and Trish went swimming in the lake? Lord knows what might have happened if Grant hadn't been there to run him off."

"I'll be okay," Cammie said urgently, premonition and anticipation and dread rolling up her spine. "Really, Mom. Only two incidents in the fifteen years you've owned the place aren't reason enough to get worried about me. I'm a big girl. I can take care of myself."

"I know. I know. But still, I won't rest easy here knowing you're so isolated by yourself. Why don't you get Grant to go along?" Before Cammie could put up a fuss, she called down the table, "Grant, Cammie's taking her vacation at the cottage and I don't want her stuck in the middle of nowhere alone for two weeks. You wouldn't mind staying with her, would you? Just to make sure she's safe?"

"No!" Cammie's objection came out too loud and forceful. Dorothy turned a puzzled gaze on her while the nearby chatterers quieted to listen in. "I mean . . . well, I know Grant has several projects he's working on and it wouldn't be right for him to get behind on my account. I'll be fine, Mom, I promise."

"That's okay, Cammie," Grant said loud enough for everyone to hear. "I can take my work with me. Besides, I wouldn't mind getting away for a couple of weeks myself."

"There, it's all settled," Dorothy pronounced. "You can have your vacation, Grant can take one with you, and I won't have to worry."

"But, Mom—"

"Yes?"

What could she say? Nothing without raising suspicion.

"Umm . . . thanks. I'll get the key before I leave."

Grant sent a smile of supreme satisfaction her way. She deflected it with a discreet scowl. They were going to have this out, and good, as soon as she got him alone.

When dusk settled in, Cammie was finally able to extricate herself from the hellacious gathering held in her honor.

"Are you sure you can't stay the night?" Dorothy asked. "Tomorrow we could do a fitting on your new outfit."

"Thanks, Mom. You and Dad went to a great deal of work to have the party, and it means a lot to me. But frankly, I'm really beat. It's been a hectic week, and if I stay I'll be up half the night visiting."

"You're right about not getting any rest here, and you sure look like you could use some. Just be careful on the road."

Cammie performed all the ritual hugs and kisses, anxious to get away.

"I love you both. You've done so much for me, I could never pay you back."

"Why, Cammie," Edward said, "there's nothing to pay back. You've been a gift to us from the day the Lord brought you here. You make us proud, and this family wouldn't be the same without you."

"That's right," Dorothy echoed. She dabbed at her eyes and added, "Sometimes I feel guilty for thinking it, and my heart hurts for you that you lost your family . . . but Cammie, Lord forgive me for saying it, but I've always been thankful your grandparents had already passed on. If they'd been alive, or if your folks had had brothers or sisters, they would have gotten you instead of us. I know it's a selfish thing to admit, but it's the truth."

Cammie's throat swelled too tight to say anything, so she hugged her parents fiercely before climbing into her car and waving good-bye. She was too distressed to realize she was speeding off with uncharacteristic carelessness.

Less than three miles away, the oil light flashed a reminder. "Damn," she screamed at the car, then pulled to the side of the road and pounded the dash in frustration.

Quelling the urge to slump against the steering wheel and give in to a crying jag, she shoved open the door and proceeded to dig out a few cans of oil from the oversized trunk.

Efficiently, she raised the hood and reached for the oil cap. She immediately snatched her hand from the overheated metal, shaking it back and forth while tears, sparked more by her pummeled emotions than by the minor burn, stung her eyes.

She found an old rag and opened the cap with enough force to twist the transmission out, then poured the oil in.

"You'd better start, you old battle-ax, or you're junk metal next week." She shoved the hood down and cleaned up the mess, unable to care about her white party dress. "I'll sleep in here if I have to, but I'm *not* going back," she vowed, and twisted the key in the ignition.

The engine growled in protest but kicked in, just as a pair of headlights rounded the corner.

The Porsche raced past, then squealed to an abrupt halt before she could hit the accelerator. Grant backed up in a millisecond, throwing dust and gravel against both cars as he blocked her path. Without bothering to cut the engine, he got out of his car and strode over to her.

Before she knew what was happening, he had flung her door open. "Get out," he ordered.

"I'm not getting out. I'm going home, Grant. Now move your car out of my way. We're going to talk, but it's not going to be here."

"Well, at least we agree about one thing." His fingers bit into her upper arms, and she pushed at him as he hauled her out of the front seat and pressed her against the side of the car. "Talking's not what I want to do here either. What I've got in mind is a little lesson for sneaking off without a word."

"You—you were busy," she stammered lamely.

"Don't insult my intelligence with that crap." His face lowered to hers as he gritted out, "Now shut up and quit running. Your *brother* wants his good-night kiss."

Seven

Her mouth opened. Whether Cammie meant to protest or welcome him—which was doubtful—he wasn't sure. Grant only knew he wasn't one to let opportunity pass him twice.

Seizing the access she had unwittingly offered, he quickly fit his mouth over hers. He heard her soft gasp of surprise mingle with his immediate groan of intimacy found. Her lips were warm and malleable and he relished them with a connoisseur's sensitivity—learning their shape and texture and taste, the way he could work them beneath his.

The shape of her bowed upper lip fit the tip of his tongue to such perfection, he was certain the small, sexy groove had been made for him and him alone.

He'd always wondered if her lips were as lush and ripe as he imagined. They weren't—they far exceeded his dreams. Sweet as peach nectar, they were meant to be savored, sipped, yet he could barely control his insatiable need to devour each succulent drop.

He could tell she was fighting herself, trying valiantly not to give in to the kiss. Her fists were still clenched and pushing against his chest while her mouth simply allowed his exploration. It maddened him, drove his urgency on to trample her damnable reserve.

"Kiss me back," he demanded. "Open your mouth and make love to mine."

"No," she groaned, "no . . ."

Wedging his tongue between her slightly parted lips, he tasted her shallowly, then more deeply, probing the hidden softness of the moist, tender interior flesh. He pushed against the straight slick teeth that stood guardian, refusing his tongue, which demanded total possession.

He was aware of the moment her fists relaxed and lay flat against his chest, then grasped his shirt. The moan of surrender came next, her teeth parting, giving up their guard.

Now that he knew she wanted it as badly as he did, Grant forced his mouth away, rejoicing in her murmur of protest. He skimmed his teeth over her chin and down the delicious length of her neck, feeling the vibration of her sigh of arousal roll wantonly from her throat.

"Please . . . Grant, *please*."

He lifted his head and stared down at her through slitted eyes, his emotional hunger, his arousal approaching pain. Her own eyes were glazed and her mouth was still wet and swollen from his kiss.

"If you want it," he whispered hoarsely, "take it."

For an uncertain moment that crackled with tension, they stared at each other.

With a cry of defeat, of triumph, she dug her fingers into his shoulders and urgently pulled him down. He vaguely realized through the pounding inside his head that if Cammie's mouth had been intoxicating before, when she gave wholly it was nirvana, paradise spiked with just enough wickedness to send him plummeting over the edge.

"More," he whispered urgently as her tongue darted into his mouth. "I need *more*."

She gave it. First hesitantly, then with a swift and eager abandon, she stroked deeply, thoroughly, learning his mouth with a grace that bordered on decadence. Then she withdrew, coaxing his tongue along the path of hers and into the haven of her mouth.

For him, it seemed a welcome, a homecoming at long last. While she molded herself along his length and ran her hands over his back, he gave in to the impulse to ravage, to be tender, to demand and to give what was the essence of all they were now, had been, and were yet to be.

Touching her breasts, stroking up her thighs and over her buttocks to tilt her into his straining hardness . . . Yes, it seemed the most natural thing in the world. He led her hand down his chest, urging it lower, lower, until, groaning in unsated need, he pressed her palm over his fly and curled her fingers into his groin.

Nothing seemed to matter except for hurtling aside the obstacles life had thrown in their path. And with each rhythmic grasp of her hand, each desperate thrust of his hips, he could feel her reaching out to him, drawing closer to the loneliness and desperation she had created, where she had held him prisoner with no hope for escape.

Now he was pulling her in with him, determined to make her fall so fast and deep that *nothing* could compete with a lifetime together. Not family. Not moral conventions. *Nothing*.

They were breathing erratically, the sound mingling with the early fall breeze, which smelled of crisp leaves and memories of fireplace smoke. They were somewhere composed of the senses, the deserted road, and two running cars long forgotten. The anticipation was unbearable; he unsnapped his jeans.

"Undo them," he whispered roughly, then led her fingers to the zipper's metal. She stiffened. "Cammie, I *need* you to touch me. I'm going out of my mind with the need."

"I . . . Grant, I—I can't." She looked quickly away. Even in the darkness he thought he spied tears.

"Can't?" he repeated in frustration and confusion. Weren't those her exact words before? "What do you mean, *can't*? Is there something wrong?"

"No," she denied quickly. "I mean . . . it's too soon."

"A minute ago it wasn't. A minute ago we were both ready to fall into the backseat and finish what we'd started with the kind of touching that's a lot more intimate than your hand stroking me."

She tried to pull away but he refused, anchoring her hand firmly against his unsheathed erection.

"We shouldn't be doing this here," she protested more urgently. "Someone could drive by any minute."

Grant could feel his frustration gather a measure of anger. More than that, he had an uneasy feeling, something niggling at him, telling him that whatever was wrong, there was more than met the eye. Cammie was sensitive; she would never play the tease. It took more than a little discipline to shut out his raging instincts and probe at the cause rather than focus on the symptoms—but he managed it.

"Does the thought of touching me repel you for some reason?"

"No! No, Grant, how could you ever think that?"

"Believe me, I don't *want* to think it. I'm just trying to understand what's going on. Talk to me, Cammie. Tell me what's wrong."

He tilted her face into the moonlight when she would have looked away. The sympathy he felt for her then overrode the dwindling urgency to take her no matter what.

"I don't want to talk about it, Grant. Let it go for tonight. Today was one of the most horrible days of my life, and I'm so drained it's all I can do to stand on my feet. Some other time, Grant, but not tonight."

He studied her awhile, touched, concerned by the silent plea he read in her eyes. "Okay, we'll drop it. Under one condition."

"That depends. Your conditions are usually stacked in your favor."

"Usually," he agreed. "But in this case, it's in both our interests." He leaned in closer and stroked the hair from her face, smiling as he touched his gift. He'd delighted giving her a lover's gift and doing it for everyone to see.

"The condition is, once we're at the cabin, we talk about anything, everything, and mostly about us."

She suddenly grasped his hands and fixed him with a stern, uncompromising stare.

"You're not going, Grant. I want you to tell Mom and Dad tomorrow that you've changed your mind."

"You've got to be kidding." He'd wondered how long it would take her to get around to it. "Give up two weeks alone with no outside interference? What do you take me for, Cammie? A fool?"

"You're nobody's fool, but neither am I. I *need* this time alone, Grant. I can't think straight as long as you're around."

"I don't want you to think straight. Look at what it got me, leaving you all alone to think this past week. Nothing but six sleepless nights while you decided I wanted you for a sleazy fling."

"That's *not* what I—"

Her heated defense was cut short by a set of headlights aimed in their direction. Grant squinted against the blinding brightness, glad for once that they'd been interrupted.

The car slowed, then pulled up beside them. Aunt Mabel rolled down her window.

"Grant, Cammie, what are you doing here?"

"I had car trouble," Cammie answered. "Grant was helping me out."

"Oh, dear. Should we go back and get—"

"No," Grant cut in smoothly. "Thanks for the offer, Aunt Mabel, but we've taken care of it. We were just about to drive back into Austin. I'm following her to make sure she gets home safe. Right, Cammie?"

"Uh . . . ." Her gaze darted from Aunt Mabel to him. "Right."

Aunt Mabel regarded them for a moment, seeming to come to the realization that Grant's hand was clamped onto the back of Cammie's neck and that she was fidgeting nervously. She gave them an odd, considering once-over, then nodded.

"Be careful then. We'll see you soon."

The minute the car took off, Cammie whirled to face him, anxiety and agitation stamped on her features.

"Did you see that? Did you see the way she looked at us?"

"Yes," he replied without inflection. "And we'll

get a lot more looks like that, too, once you decide you've got the guts to come out of the closet."

"I don't believe you. How can you be so flippant, so—"

"How can *you* be so negligent with your safety?" he inserted, deliberately ignoring the direction she was headed. "When I drove up you *were* having car problems, weren't you? I swear, Cammie. Sometimes I could shake you for leaving your door unlocked or driving in something so undependable. Do you have any idea what it would do to me if anything ever happened to you?"

"Forget the car," she retorted. "We're not through talking about my lack of guts." She shoved a finger into his chest while her voice shook with fury. "Maybe that's true, but at least I don't beat up other people's feelings while I only think about myself."

Grant's jaw clenched and worked back and forth several times. Don't blow your cool, he ordered himself. Stay in control, and work this to your advantage.

"I'll follow you to make sure you get home okay," he said tightly. "Once we're there we can talk. Or we can *not* talk while you don't tell me why you can't bring yourself to touch me. That, and why I'm such a selfish SOB for thinking I should have the right to be in love with a woman who's so afraid of hurting other people's feelings she uses them to keep from facing her own."

Cammie stepped back as though he'd struck her. He felt bad about it, but then again he wanted her enough to be brutal, if that's what it took. The battle had started. He intended to win—for richer or poorer, in sickness and in health, and even in death, not to part.

"How can you say something that . . . that—"

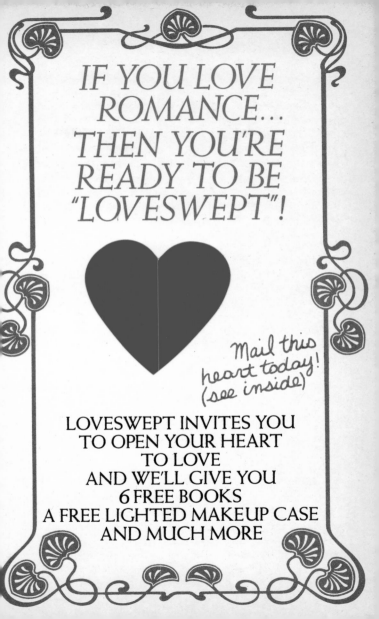

OPEN YOUR HEART TO LOVE
YOU'LL BE LOVESWEPT WITH THIS FREE OFFER

HERE'S WHAT YOU GET:

1. **FREE!** SIX NEW LOVESWEPT NOVELS! You get 6 beautiful stories filled with passion, romance, laughter, and tears... exciting romances to stir the excitement of falling in love... again and again.

2. **FREE!** A BEAUTIFUL MAKEUP CASE WITH A MIRROR THAT LIGHTS UP!
What could be more useful than a makeup case with a mirror that lights up*? Once you open the tortoise-shell finish case, you have a choice of brushes... for your lips, your eyes, and your blushing cheeks.

*(batteries not included)

3. **SAVE!** MONEY-SAVING HOME DELIVERY! Join the Loveswept at-home reader service and we'll send you 6 new novels each month. You always get 15 days to preview them before you decide. Each book is yours for only $2.09 — a savings of 41¢ per book.

4. BEAT THE CROWDS! You'll always receive your Loveswept books before they are available in bookstores. You'll be the first to thrill to these exciting new stories.

BE LOVESWEPT TODAY — JUST COMPLETE, DETACH AND MAIL YOUR FREE-OFFER CARD.

FREE – LIGHTED MAKEUP CASE!
FREE – 6 LOVESWEPT NOVELS!

- NO OBLIGATION
- NO PURCHASE NECESSARY

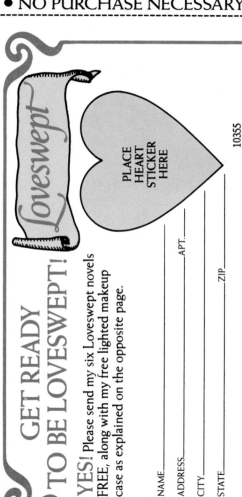

REMEMBER!

- The free books and gift are mine to keep!
- There is no obligation!
- I may preview each shipment for 15 days!
- I can cancel anytime!

(DETACH AND MAIL CARD TODAY.)

"Honest?" He gave her a slight push toward her car, then headed back to his own. "Meet you at the house. We'll pick it up there."

Cammie was still seething by the time she opened her front door. Seething, fearful, and a total mess. She wanted to curse him for making her life so miserable. She also wanted to love him.

Grant never let a question go unanswered. She'd always admired his analytical nature, yet this time her admiration was laced with apprehension. She wanted to embrace the potential healing he offered while she shrank from the fear of failure.

Yes, she had failed the challenge tonight, unable to take the leap. But he hadn't belittled her. His anger emerged because he was in love with her and she couldn't rise to *that* challenge. His eyes told her that now as she dropped into an over-stuffed chair—rather than beside him on the couch.

He sat forward, silent a moment, his fingers forming a contemplative steeple.

"You can't go with me, Grant," she said.

"Oh?" He raised a brow. "That's news to me. The way I see it, I *can* and I *am*, whether you like it or not."

"Then you go alone, without me."

"You're already committed."

"I'll uncommit then."

"Good luck." His lips formed a mocking smile. "Let me know what kind of excuse you come up with, because it's going to have to be something pretty amazing to convince the folks you've got a legitimate reason not to go along with me. Especially since I'm inclined to ask a lot of questions."

"You wouldn't."

"Try me." His eyes narrowed in challenge. "I'm holding the ace, Cammie. And you should know by now that I never bluff."

"I thought I knew you all these years, Grant. But I was wrong. You don't play fair. You make up the rules to suit your purposes."

"That's right, darlin'. I've always played to win. You were just too blinded by what you wanted to see to find out what I really am."

"Which in this case is conniving, despicable, arrogant, and . . . and . . ." She searched for another insult to throw into his smug, satisfied face. "Insensitive," she finished.

"I'm also head over heels in love." His eyes met hers evenly, but with enough force to knock the world from beneath her feet. His determined expression blended with his words to tilt the scales in favor of his skewed point of view.

"As for those newer qualities you seem to have discovered in me," he went on, "I've probably been all those things at one time or another. But I'm also honest. You have my word on it, Cammie. I'll fight as dirty as I have to, to get what I want. Consider yourself warned, because I won't stop for anyone or anything. Not until I hear you say that you're in love with me too. Too crazy in love to give a tinker's damn about what anyone else thinks because you're committed to me, and only me. Sorry to break the news, but I happen to be insufferably selfish as well. Skimpy, guilty, stolen bits and pieces of you won't cut it. I want your loyalty, I want your body, I want your heart. I refuse to accept anything less."

For a moment she struggled with a mixture of panic and excitement. As a brother, Grant was someone she had relied on for comfort and understanding. She couldn't reconcile that with this dark stranger he had evolved into. This man who was formidable, challenging . . . dangerous.

She felt like she was in over her head, scrambling to salvage the crumbling remains of her old world. Her dearest ally had become her second opponent. The biggest enemy was someone she didn't recognize inside herself. With too many mixed emotions roiling inside her, she felt she was in both hell and heaven, with no way to tell one from the other.

In a last-ditch effort to cling to the familiar, to the safety of what they'd had, she said honestly, "I do love you, Grant. I've always loved you."

"Not good enough. I want you to be *in* love with me." His gaze roved over her face, down to her breasts, then lingered at her lap, a heavy-lidded gaze that was laden with sexuality. "You're flushed. Your nipples are tight. You want me. That's not good enough, either."

She slid, like a drowning man going under, into the inky blackness that beckoned. Cammie swallowed hard, wet her lips.

Grant leaned forward. With the propriety of a husband, he stroked his fingertips over her breast, then casually withdrew.

She ached to call him back, to plead for more. But she didn't dare.

"Tell me, Cammie," he whispered, "are you in love with me?"

Was she? Oh, Lord, she didn't know. It was too much, too soon, and too possibly true.

"We can't forget the people we love," she said, frantic to remember what stood between them.

Clasping the locket tight, she scanned the room for portraits, for handmade reminders of why she couldn't do this, shouldn't even think it. He was steering her on a one-way course of no return, and she flailed blindly against the tide.

"That again," he snorted impatiently. "Damn, why do you always have to go back to that?"

"Because it's there, Grant. It exists and it won't go away. You've never lost a family. I *have*. It's torture. It's the most horrible, excruciating thing in my life. Your family is all that I've got and you're asking me to risk giving it up. If you love me the way you say you do, how can you expect me to go through that again?"

"How? I'll tell you *how*. While you've been coping with torture, I've been living in agony. What do you think it's done to *me*? Watching other men touch you in a way I never could, seeing an engagement ring on your finger while I had to cough up a hearty 'congratulations,' when it was all I could do not to puke it made me so sick. Can you imagine what *that* was like?"

"No." Unwillingly, her heart hurt for him while the bitterness in his voice flailed her. "No, I never knew. You never let it show."

"Well, now you know. You lost your family, and those are wounds that can never heal. But my wounds go deep, too, Cammie. While you were getting on with your life, I had to watch from the sidelines without a snowball's chance in hell of competing. It was killing me by inches. The success, the women, the man who had it all . . . God, what a joke." He laughed harshly. "I couldn't have the only thing I really wanted. Without you, all I had meant nothing."

The enormity of his emotional need stunned her, and also stoked a yearning in her to appease the hunger she had created. His honesty had unshrouded the deepest place in her heart. The place she had buried along with her loved ones, that was so empty and aching she couldn't bear to take it out, examine it, and brave the chance of ever losing the emotional distance that kept her safe—*and* forever alone.

His eyes burned into hers without apology, with a stark rawness that could only be satisfied with a melding of their souls. With total possession of each other's hearts. With a physical mating of primal intensity.

His need was absolute. It frightened her. And she hated her cowardice.

Take the chance, came the whisper from the depths of unearthed need. *If you take it, it's all or nothing and you've got no guarantees*, countered the voice of reason. The echo of fear mocked her without pity: *If it doesn't work, you could lose more than family, more than your heart. To give him what he wants means reopening the scab. It's a wound you're so afraid to comfort, it keeps on running . . . just the same as you.*

The past gaped open like a yawning abyss. She felt herself teetering, the sensation akin to vertigo. It was too much like hearing a scratch coming from the inside of a coffin. Creeping closer to it, compelled to know what lay within, and yet terrified to discover what might reach out from the other side of darkness. Life? Or something ominous, a nightmare waiting to justify her fear?

"What you want is more than I can give, Grant." Her heart sank at the sound of her own words.

"No." He stood and reached for her. She couldn't stop her trembling as he pulled her to her feet, and he made it worse by running his hands over her arms, twining his fingers through her hair, then locking her body against his. "It's not that you *can't*. Because you *will*. It's only a matter of time."

"How can you be so sure?"

"Because I know you better than anyone else. Sometimes, I think, better than you know yourself. And because when I hold you, your body gives me the very promises you're fighting so hard to deny."

It was true, and she knew it. She was losing the battle. It was only a matter of time before she could no longer hide—from him, or herself. Grant had opened a door long shut. She had dared to peek, and had quickly retreated.

But now it would haunt her, the ghosts she'd glimpsed and the knowledge of what could be, if only she was strong and courageous enough to take the risk.

She looked into his face, a face of honesty, of depth, and character. She looked into the face of a man she was falling in love with, a man she was only now coming to know.

"Kiss me, Grant." The words came naturally, with a rightness that surprised her. Just to make sure, she gathered her courage and said again, "Kiss me now . . . hard and long and deep."

Eight

"Thank you for joining us. We hope to see you again tomorrow at six and ten. This is Cammie Walker . . ."

"And this is Russ Aberdeen, saying—"

"Good night," they said in unison.

Cammie kept her professional smile firmly in place until the floor manager signaled they were off the air.

"Whew," she breathed, letting her mouth relax. "What a night, huh, big guy?"

"You can say that again," Russ agreed readily. "What say we wrap up and blow this pop stand?"

"Sounds good to me." Pushing her chair back she got up and stretched. "Sure you don't mind giving me a lift home?"

"Hey, are you kidding? This is the closest I've gotten to making points with you."

She laughed. "Get outta here. I swear, if I have one more problem with that car, I'm in the market for a new one. The repairs would have been finished today except they had to scrounge for prehistoric parts. But at least the mechanic promised I'd have my wheels back by tomorrow."

"Darn," Russ said, grinning. "Maybe I can shove some bribe money under the table and get that extended a few days."

"Save your money, Russ, and spend it on one of your many fans."

"Which unfortunately doesn't include you," he said wryly.

While they finished up, Cammie reflected that she missed this kind of lighthearted banter with Grant. Was it possible they could recapture an essence of the old days once they were alone at the cottage?

They were making the short trip together—not that she hadn't had second thoughts. After picking up the phone twice, she'd dialed their parents' number, then hung up before it could ring. Not only had she decided she couldn't get out of the situation without making waves, in her heart of hearts, she knew she didn't want to.

She was making progress, she told herself. At least she'd been honest enough to admit she wanted this time alone with him. Unwise as it was, as much as it still terrified her, she wanted it.

"What've you got planned for your vacation, Cammie?" Russ asked as they walked through the parking lot together.

"Some much-needed R&R, Russ," she answered, knowing rest and relaxation was probably the last purpose this vacation would serve. Her mind immediately shied away from the possibilities that awaited her.

"Cammie. Stop."

She turned at the sound of Grant's voice while Russ unlocked the passenger side of his car. It coincided with a loud *thud* as Grant nearly slammed his own door shut.

"Grant! What are you doing here?" Her heart went into double time while her stomach decided to catch butterflies.

His towering presence loomed over her and Russ, who was shorter by several inches and a good fifty pounds lighter. Grant stared from one to the other until Cammie reached up self-consciously to smooth down her hair, while last night's parting kiss shot sparks through her memory.

"I thought you might need a ride home," he said in a tight voice.

"That's okay," Russ said. "I promised Cammie a ride home already. You're Grant Kennedy, Cammie's brother, aren't you? I think we met at a station party last Christmas. Nice seeing you again." He offered his hand.

Grant stared at it with ill-disguised antagonism before gripping it in a bone-crushing shake. Russ's smile wavered uncertainly while he tried to disengage himself from the overt warning.

Cammie stared speechless as several tense seconds ticked by. Grant was jealous! She'd never seen him glare at someone with open hostility before. The realization was . . . flattering. Just as his behavior toward her co-worker was totally out of line.

"My car wasn't fixed yet, so Russ offered me a ride home," she explained quickly, trying to defuse the situation.

"How kind." Grant released Russ's hand and draped a proprietary arm over her shoulders. "I'll take Cammie home. We have vacation plans to discuss."

Russ stared long and consideringly, absorbing

the implicit intimacy in Grant's gesture. Anxiety coiled tight inside Cammie.

After a moment, Russ shrugged. "Sorry. I didn't realize it was a family affair."

"It's not!" she automatically denied, desperate to end the awkward scene. Grant's hand slid down to her waist and pulled her close; Russ's eyes followed the movement. Good heavens, she thought, what kind of conclusions was he drawing?

The obvious ones, of course, she admitted to herself.

"Um . . . Russ. Grant's not exactly my brother," she said hastily. She could almost feel Grant's smile of satisfaction with the admission. "I mean . . . I'm adopted and—"

"Enough said." Russ took a step back. "I don't mean to stare. I just wasn't expecting my competition to be so close to home."

Cammie clenched and unclenched the fabric of her skirt, forcing herself not to make any more flustered excuses. By tomorrow night, her private life would be public knowledge. It made her uneasy, wondering what kind of gossip would spread behind her back.

"Then I'm glad to set the record straight." Grant parted on that note, pulling her in the direction of his parked car. Cammie hazarded a nervous backward glance at Russ, who was openly scrutinizing them.

"See you tomorrow night, Russ," she managed to say around the knot of anxiety in her throat. Then she quickened her pace to keep up with Grant's lengthening strides.

Once they were mercifully alone in his car, Cammie leaned her head back and took several deep breaths, trying to still the awful sense of fatality welling within her. Facing Grant as he revved the engine, she gazed reproachfully at him.

"What in heaven's name got into you?" she demanded. "You managed quite a scene in front of someone I have to work with daily, Grant."

"Damn right," he said tautly. "And I'd like to know what got into *you.* Twenty-four hours ago I was the only man on your agenda, and tonight I catch you getting into a car with some jerk who's got the hots for you."

"He's my co-anchor, for heaven's sake!"

"Who also happens to have other things on his mind besides the news."

"Quit being ridiculous."

Grant peeled out of the parking lot with a muttered curse. "You told me a month ago he was hitting on you. And if you think I'm about to let anyone move in on my territory, you'd better think again."

Cammie reflexively pressed her foot into the floorboard as he rounded a sharp curve.

"That doesn't give you the right to make my work relations strained," she said. "What am I supposed to say when the secret's out?"

"Then it's no longer a secret, which suits me fine. I doubt we'll rate a headline on your broadcast, so I suggest you simply tell them it's none of their business, or better yet, tell them the truth. They can like it or lump it, and let it go at that."

"Easy for you to say. The only person you have to work around is yourself."

"You're right," he said as the Porsche came to an abrupt halt in her driveway. He turned to her and pinned her with a steely gaze. "It *is* easy for me to say. *Cammie Walker is the only woman in my life and in no way is she my sister.* Nothing would give me more pleasure than to announce that to the whole world. I'm proud to be with you, Cammie. It hurts me to think that you're ashamed to be with me."

"I'm not ashamed of you, Grant!"

"No? You could've fooled me."

She held his unwavering gaze for several seconds before she was compelled to look away. Grant was right. She had implied by her words, her actions, that she was ashamed of their relationship.

Now she felt ashamed of herself.

Staring at her clasped hands, she said quietly, "I . . . I'm still struggling to come to terms with all the changes we've gone through. I don't know where we're headed yet, Grant. Until I do, I think it's best to be discreet."

"I know," he said slowly. "I keep reminding myself I've had a lot longer to think about this than you have. It's not easy, but I promise to try to be more patient."

He hooked a finger beneath her chin and tilted her face into the dappled moonlight. His smile was tender.

"I'll call you the next time I need a ride." She knew her simple statement was yet another step forward.

"You'd better. Otherwise I'm apt to throw another jealous fit."

They laughed quietly together, and oh, it felt so good. To laugh with Grant was a part of life she needed. Especially now.

He kissed her good night, and it was rich.

She fell asleep with the memory, a smile of happiness still tinging her lips.

Cammie laid an extra pair of jeans into the suitcase, next to a few sweaters and T-shirts. The weather was still too uncertain to know if the cold spell would hold or give way to a final blast of heat.

Going to her dresser, she debated over lingerie. Usually she slept in an oversized dorm shirt Grant had given her several Christmases ago, and she'd packed that. What she was staring at now was a sheer red nightgown she'd bought for a honeymoon that had never come to pass.

To take it was to admit she intended to sleep with him.

Not to take it was to salve her conscience and feed herself a line of tripe that she was going to control the escalating desire.

"Ready, Cammie?"

She jumped and spun around to face him. Grant framed the doorway of her bedroom. He hadn't been in since that fateful morning.

"I didn't hear you knock."

"Obviously. I let myself in. But as agreed, I'm waiting for an invitation before I come any farther."

He chuckled and grinned seductively, his gaze trailing to the bed.

Her heart pounded. She nervously wet her lips.

"Some groceries are in the kitchen," she said. "You get those while I finish packing."

"Done," he said agreeably before pushing away from the door frame. Just as she turned back to the dresser, he poked his head around the corner. "Don't forget your red nightie, Cammie."

She snatched back the hand that hovered over the nightgown and whirled to face him, but saw only his retreating back. His laughter echoed in the hallway.

"Ohhh, that *man*," she grumbled, even as an unbidden smiled tugged at her lips.

Before she let herself think too hard, she

grabbed the nightgown and added it to the suitcase. The silk was appropriately scarlet, she
thought. With her cheeks competing in color
scheme, she quickly stuffed the gown beneath
more respectable attire.

It wasn't that she was going to bed with him, she
told herself as she clicked the latches shut. It was
just that she'd paid an arm and a leg for the thing
and she might as well get some use out of it.

Right.

Outside, she set her bag next to his car and
waited while he put aside the groceries and opened
the trunk.

"I could have gotten that for you, Cammie."

"So you could take a peek?" She shifted, still
uneasy about her dubious motives.

He chuckled while he hoisted the suitcase into
the trunk.

When he was through loading up, she turned
toward the passenger door, but he stopped her
with a firm grip on both arms.

"What's wrong?" he asked.

"Nothing. Just . . . nothing."

"Is it Russ? Is it still strained at work?"

"No. He's fine. He told us to have a good time.
Work's almost . . . normal again."

"But you're nervous. How come?"

"I'm not nervous. I'm just . . . ready to hit the
road."

"Is that why you've hardly looked at me since I
got here?" He tilted his head until she couldn't
avoid meeting his questioning gaze. "We're not
hitting the road until you spill it."

"Okay," she sighed in exasperation. "I'm nervous. Now can we go?"

"What do you think I've got planned, Cammie?
An attack the minute we get there?"

"I—I—" She stuttered to a halt. For heaven's sake, she was a grown woman, she thought. She should start acting like one. "I honestly don't know what to expect, Grant," she admitted, relieved to get her doubts into the open. "And I'm afraid I'm making a big mistake by going through with this."

"By *this*, you mean taking a vacation together?"

"You know that's not what I mean."

"You're right. I know that's not what you mean. Look, Cammie, we both realize there's a possibility we'll sleep together. I pray that we do. But that's not going to happen unless you want it as much as I do. So relax. We'll take it one day at a time. Okay?"

He gave her an encouraging smile, then tweaked her nose in a familiar, affectionate gesture. Cammie felt the tenseness in her shoulders ebb away, along with her guard.

"Okay," she agreed. "Ready to go fishin', partner?"

"Partner," he repeated, pleased he'd derailed her early retreat. It was important to keep her defenses down so he could solidify his hold. "I like the sound of that," he added in a deceptively benign voice, meant to lure her deeper into a sense of security.

"Bet I can catch more than you," she challenged.

"You always catch more than me." He laughed easily and studied her in the early-morning light, imagining what she'd look like at daybreak snuggled up to him in one of the cottage beds. "Of course, if I didn't spend so much time baiting your hook, I might give you a run for your money."

"Worms." She made a face, as she slipped into her seat. "Yech. Slimy little suckers. They give me the creeps."

Grant leaned into her side of the car as she looked down to fasten her seat belt.

"What say we trade jobs this year? I'll fry the fish if you'll gut them."

"What!" Cammie swung around, her face instantly a breath away from his.

Her eyes widened; her breath caught sharp and fast.

Grant smiled, elated by her response. He lingered, holding the closeness until he was sure she expected a kiss.

Straightening back up, he winked mischievously.

"Okay," he said, "I'll gut and scale. But we both do the dishes and split the chores."

He strode around to the driver's side, whistling. Judging from Cammie's expression, she was eager for that kiss. Good thing, because within two weeks he intended to add making up the same bed to their domestic routine.

Nine

Grant stared up at the ceiling, fighting the urge to storm into the next room, where he could hear Cammie tossing in bed.

One day at a time, he'd said. The first day had been easy enough, airing out the small cedar cottage, putting up groceries, wandering down to the lake. He'd kept his hands in check, determined to woo Cammie slowly, purposefully.

After all, they had two weeks, and she seemed to be happy with the lack of pressure. He'd promised patience, knowing she deserved it . . . but, hell, he was only human.

By the time day two rolled into day three, he was taking cold swims. Being this close with no one around was too tempting, straining his passions to the breaking point. He felt like he deserved a gold medal for self-restraint.

Holding hands, taking walks, having long conversations, sharing silences and lingering gazes were wonderful, needed. But they weren't nearly enough. He'd taken great pains to guide them on a path meant to lead to the altar. Apparently, in all his good thinking, he'd miscalculated somewhere.

He'd abstained from pushing Cammie into intimacy, hoping she would become impatient and take some initiative. She hadn't. Neither had their heart-to-heart talks led to any confessions about the unbroached subject that pulsed between them. The subject that pulsed even now between his legs and that she had yet to touch.

Today was day seven and his patience was out. He was starved for kisses—hot and wet. Keeping them almost chaste had been self-induced torture, but he knew he couldn't trust himself to stop there forever.

He was driving himself crazy just thinking about it. Since it was too late to go for a swim, he dropped to the floor and began a brisk set of push-ups.

"Eighty . . . ninety . . . one hundred."

He groaned and lay flat on the floor, letting the cool wood cushion his cheek. But all he could think of was her skin, just as smooth, only soft and warm.

A lot of good the push-ups had done. He was so hard he was hurting. Every time he'd pressed down he'd imagined entering her with the same rhythmic thrust.

Tomorrow. Yes, tomorrow he would take the reins and guide them in a more intimate direction. In the meantime he wasn't getting any sleep.

He reached for a pair of jeans. Not bothering to zip them up, he padded toward the kitchen. He stopped at Cammie's bedroom door, which was cracked open.

An invitation? Not likely. He took it as a sign of the trust he had built over the past week. All was quiet and he assumed Cammie had found the sleep that eluded him.

For several moments he stood there, debating. Could he look and not touch? She wouldn't know, and what would be the harm in watching her a few minutes, filling his senses with the sight of her in the bed he longed to be in?

He quietly pushed the door open, then slowly, soundlessly, walked to the bed. Moonlight spilled over her, and a cool breeze filtered into the room from the open window.

Cammie was breathing evenly, her eyes were shut. His gaze roved over her hungrily, lovingly. Unexpectedly, she raised her lids and stared straight at him.

For a moment, neither spoke, but both felt the sudden tug-of-war tension, a pull between them that filled up the room.

"I couldn't sleep," he whispered.

Cammie swallowed hard. She couldn't move. She couldn't keep her eyes from following the path of his bare chest down to the deep, open V of his unfastened jeans. She could see the dark wiry gathering of his pubic hair, and it stirred an answering sensuality in the depths of her femininity.

For days—that had seemed like years—she had been struggling with the gathering need to touch Grant, to feel his hands in her hair, gliding sure and unhindered over her body. He'd been so damnably careful in his affections, she had been fighting the urge to scream in frustration.

"Neither could I," she finally answered. Forcing her clenched hands from beneath the sheet, she lay one atop it. Her movements felt stiff, apprehensive—and compelled. She reached for his hand.

He hesitated a moment, then sat on the edge of the bed. It creaked with his weight. He laid her palm against his thigh, pressing down lightly. She couldn't control the quickening of her heart. The feel of him was so good, so wanted, it was all she could do not to pull him down beside her.

"Think maybe we're awake for the same reason?" he asked in a low, mesmerizing voice as he stroked the hair away from her face.

"That depends on the reason," she said, willing her own voice not to shake.

"I want you." His eyes darkened, his features tightened with restraint. "But I'm trying really hard to give you some time and to take it slow."

"I know." She smiled her appreciation for his efforts, when all she wanted to do was cry her frustration for his maddening discipline and her own inability to break the barriers that still held her captive. That prevented her from confessing them even now. "You've been the perfect gentleman," she said instead.

His jaw locked tight. "It's wearing thin, Cammie."

"Is it?" She wondered if he'd heard the edge of hope in her voice.

He looked at her hard, his eyes probing hers with all pretense of politeness stripped away.

"We've done a lot of talking, but not about the things that are keeping me from climbing between these sheets."

Could she tell him? Could she do it *now*? And could she do it knowing that the runaway emotions coursing between them would escalate and could never be pushed back?

Taking a deep breath, she rushed forward.

"I have a problem. And it's not just Mom and Dad."

She heard the deep exhalation of his breath just before he leaned down until his chest hovered over hers. His hands cupped her face, and she saw his relief, his understanding.

"I've been waiting for this. Tell me, Cammie. Tell me what keeps you from me."

"I don't understand it all myself, Grant."

"Then maybe we could understand it together."

With a sob, she reached for him, wrapping her arms tightly around his shoulders. "Hold me, Grant. Please, hold me. I've always needed you, everything you are to me. But I've never needed you so much as I do now."

"Cammie," he groaned. "Oh, Lord, Cammie. I'm here. I'll always be here. I love you too much to ever let go."

He swiped the sheet to the foot of the bed, then rolled with her onto their sides, cradling her head against his chest and clasping his arms tight around her. Their legs intertwined, and she burrowed into the haven of his strength.

"You always loved me more than anyone," she whispered around the knot of tears. "More than any of the men who gave me a ring, who I thought I could marry. But I couldn't, Grant. I could never go through with a commitment. I could never get past this thing that's inside me that won't go away."

"It will," he promised. "I'll help you make it go away. And you'll never know how thankful I am that none of the others could do that. Whatever this thing is, no matter how terrible, I'm glad it was there if it kept them from having you."

She nodded, her cheek sliding wetly against the wonderful abrasion of his chest hair, the warmth of his skin beneath. She sent heavenward a silent prayer of thanks for this man who loved her, even her weaknesses and flaws, knowing she was safe in telling him anything, everything.

"They said something was wrong with me," she

whispered. "And I thought . . . I thought they were right. I even went for therapy trying to understand."

"You saw a shrink?" he asked incredulously. "You mean there was something that wrong, and you didn't tell me about it? Cammie, why didn't you talk to *me* instead of some stranger who couldn't care about you the way I do?"

"What was I going to do, Grant? Tell you I couldn't go through with a marriage because I couldn't bring myself to totally let go? That even if I was attached to someone and I said I loved them, I couldn't find it inside me to let go of the emotional distance that kept me safe? That's what the therapist said. My fiancés felt that aloofness, and they wanted some honest depth from a wife. I know you all thought I broke the engagements but twice, it was them, not me."

Cammie could feel the return of shame. She'd lied about the breakups to her family, embarrassed to have been the one spurned, and unwilling to confess the reasons.

"Maybe you didn't really love them," Grant said quietly, without reproach. "Did you think of that? Maybe it was because you were waiting for the right person and you didn't realize he was waiting for you all along."

"Maybe. But that wasn't all." As he comfortingly stroked her back, she gathered herself, seeking the courage for the most horrible revelation of all.

"I was . . . frigid. I—I'm afraid I still am. And Grant, it terrifies me. I kept trying to act like a normal woman, and all I could do was freeze up. Here were these men, decent, good men who loved me but somehow I couldn't love back, and every time I tried to go through with—with a consummation, it was . . . Oh Lord, Grant, it was horrible. Painful. Humiliating."

"*What*?" Grant strained to look at her, disbelief etched across his face.

The old humiliation surfaced anew. The cut of failure was still too incisive, and facing it when she'd worked so hard to ignore it was almost more than she could bear. Seeing his shocked expression made her want to shrink from it again, to do what she had learned to do so well—hide, pretend that what plagued her life and kept her unwhole didn't matter, when it really mattered so god-awful much.

She covered her face with her hands. Grant gripped her wrists and tried to wrest them away.

"Look at me, Cammie," he demanded. "I hate what you're doing to yourself. Look at me, *now*."

"No, no," she whimpered. "I don't want you to look at me. I'm so . . . so *screwed up*."

"Quit hiding your face from me, dammit. You're not screwed up. The only thing that's screwed up is the way you're beating yourself for something you can't help."

She let him draw her hands away then, and even when he held her chin so she had to look at him, she found the courage inside herself to meet his caring, strong, and deeply moving gaze.

"Don't ever hide from me again, Cammie," he whispered sternly. "I won't let you do it. Not to me, and not to yourself. There's nothing we can't overcome together. Do you believe me?"

Looking into his eyes—compassionate, loving, too deep for words—she could believe anything was possible. Even the impossible.

"I believe you," she said in a choked voice

He kissed away her tears. He kissed each eyelid, then pressed his lips against her forehead.

"Now I'm going to ask you some questions and I want you to be totally honest with me. Even if the answers are hard for you to say."

"All right, Grant. For myself, for you, I will." She sniffled, determined to see this through and put it behind her at long last.

"Were you ever molested?"

"No."

"When you did have sex, did you have a bad experience? Did someone hurt you or—"

"Grant, I never did. I tried . . . several times. Only the pain, I was too . . . dry. I couldn't—they couldn't—"

"Shhh, it's okay." He stroked his hand through her hair and murmured a sound of encouragement. "Did you see a doctor to find out if there was something physically wrong that could be corrected?"

"I saw a doctor. Physically I was fine. It was . . . mental. Emotional. Like a wall I couldn't scale."

"Did you talk to your therapist about it?"

Cammie nodded. "She thought it was tied up with my inability to make a commitment . . . that I had a mental block against intimacy. Because—because I had to protect myself from loss."

"Loss? Of what?"

"Of the people I love—if I let myself love them completely."

"How could you lose the people you love, Cammie?"

"I did."

Without warning, the door she had peeked into gaped wide open. Before she could shrink back, she stared, as if some unseen force had shoved her face inside her very own personalized house of horrors.

The scratch she had heard from inside the tomb was really the agonized scream of her mother; it came from the blood-splattered face of her father.

And her brother. Oh, God, no. Not her brother. Not Justin. Lying beside her, his body distorted, crushed, next to hers, his eyes wide open and staring sightlessly into hers while an exclamation of surprise froze upon his lips. But a minute ago they had been fighting over him crossing their invisible line to grab her diary and her father had turned around to make them straighten up and just then a big truck blew his horn and Daddy was over the line but it wasn't an invisible line.

And it was dark, so dark she couldn't see, she could only hear. And what she heard was a sound so awful she thought she must have died because nothing could be this bad except a nightmare.

Only it wasn't a nightmare. She was wide awake and she was staring at the severed hand of her mother, the wedding band she had loved so much smeared in her blood. And the siren . . . it was so loud it drowned out her own agonized screams. Then someone was dragging her away.

"Mama!" Cammie suddenly shrieked. "Mama, don't leave me. Don't go away. Daddy! Daddy! Where are you? Don't let them take you away from me. I'm so sorry, Justin. You can cross the line, I don't care if you read my diary. I didn't mean to yell at you. I didn't meant to make you die. I love you, I love you, I—Oh, God, take me instead. It was my fault. I didn't mean to make you die—"

"Cammie!"

She struggled against the hands holding her flailing arms, gripping her against an iron wall that swayed back and forth instead of letting her follow her family into the darkness, across to the other side.

"I want to go too," she cried. "Take me too."

She was racked with choked, heaving sobs that rushed up from the pit of hysteria. The darkness gradually receded and from a distance she heard a beloved, familiar voice crooning, "It's all right, I've got you. You're safe. Just hold tight to me."

"I killed them. It was my fault. All my fault." She wept, but she wept dryly, no tears left.

"No, baby. It wasn't your fault. It was an accident. You're safe now. You'll be all right."

"Grant?" She looked at him as though he were her salvation, trying to focus on a face she hadn't expected to see.

"I'm here," he whispered, rocking her back and forth.

"I saw it," she gasped in horror. "I kept trying not to see it, but I saw. I yelled at Justin, my father turned around, and . . . and—"

"And it *wasn't . . . your . . . fault.*"

"If I hadn't been fighting, if I hadn't—"

"*No.*" He shook her twice. His face came into better focus. "Kids fight, Cammie. Adults are responsible for controlling the car. No one blames you but yourself. Look again. Look past the nightmare. Tell me what you see."

"I—I'm alone. I'm . . . alive. But they're not."

"No, they're not. But you can't bury yourself with them. You *are* alive. You *have* to live. Nothing can bring them back."

Suddenly he ground his mouth against hers, and she could taste his flesh, her tears. He kissed her so deep and hard, it hurt. She welcomed the pain, the validation that she could *feel*.

"*This,*" he whispered sharply, "Cammie, *this* is *life.*"

He clasped her hand and pressed it firmly against his heavily pounding heart and repeated, "*This* is life."

Greedily she absorbed it—the thud of humanity, the wellspring of love and home.

Ten

Cammie stared out the kitchen window. The calico curtains framed the small panes of glass—and the image of Grant chopping wood in the clearing about twenty feet away.

She watched as he embedded the ax into a broken limb, then shucked off his plaid flannel shirt. A healthy sheen of sweat glistened over his back and the honed muscles of his shoulders and arms as he hoisted the ax once more. It arched in the air, his biceps bunched as he struck with perfect precision.

A warm, familiar glow ignited and spread in a lazy, satisfied trickle through her veins as she watched . . . and remembered.

She remembered the miracle of their bonding, of her healing. The way he held her through the emotional aftermath, and she held him in return. For two nights now they had shared the same bed, had slept peacefully and innocently in each other's arms. They had shared deep, soulful kisses, and caresses that were salve to the old but rapidly mending wounds.

Watching him now, the same sensation she had experienced the first time she'd seen him naked resurfaced. It left her needful, with a damp, aching want that was so strong, it was almost unbearable. It was torment. It was delight and reassurance that she *could* embrace the fullness of womanhood. A glance, a thought, a casual brush of his hand . . . No more was needed to tap into the dam of her sensuality that Grant had yet to partake of—except in careful, gentle, small measures.

His patience, his insight, was a tonic, nourishing her. He had given, she had taken, until she was strong enough to nourish herself. To feed her soul and fill her body with him, and to give equally in return.

The circle was complete—almost. Her fragmented life was whole—almost.

Tonight. Yes, tonight they would make love and the almosts would be no more.

The decision left her light-headed, dizzy with excitement. A little scared, but proud. Because even if she failed, she knew it would be a victory for them both.

Elated with the decision, her adrenaline pumping in anticipation, Cammie pushed away from the sink. Grabbing a can of beer on the way out, she left the cabin with a light step that didn't seem to quite touch the ground.

"Thought you might be thirsty."

Grant stopped in mid-arc as she pressed the ice-cold can between his shoulder blades. The October breeze wisped across his skin, bringing the tangy scent of sweat mingled with a fading hint of soap to her nostrils.

He looked, he smelled, he *was* the epitome of man.

Grant turned. His slow smile reached inside her heart and spread all the way down to her toes.

The excitement of his nearness, the victorious decision finally made, swirled into the vivid red and yellow leaves, raining like nature's confetti over their heads and about their feet.

Jubilant, Cammie hoisted the can up. With a mischievous smile she taunted, "You want it? You'll have to catch me first."

She took off at a fast sprint, stealing the advantage while Grant dropped the ax against the growing stack of logs. Laughing all the way, she dodged his grip and ran to the other side of the woodpile.

Grant could feel his heart accelerate, and it had nothing to do with the game of chasing Cammie. Her laughter washed over him, the spontaneity he'd missed of late a welcome assurance, a sign the time was drawing near.

"Come here, you little—" With a lunge, he grabbed for her around the side and just missed.

She moved the beer can back and forth and stuck her tongue out, the juvenile gesture unpardonably risqué for his starved sensibilities.

"Okay, folks, it's a tie and the clock is running out," she announced in a good imitation of a sportscaster. "She's got the beer, but *can* he block the touchdown—"

"*Tackle!*"

Cammie screeched in laughter as Grant knocked her to the ground, cushioning her fall with his own body. He wrestled with her while she held the can high above her head.

Pinning her down in a sea of autumn leaves, he feathered her ribs with his fingers, exactly where he knew she was the most ticklish.

"I give up! I give up! Take the beer, it's yours," she squealed in surrender.

Grant took the can and popped open the top. Conjuring up his most menacing expression, he tipped it forward a fraction.

"You're gonna pay for this, Cammie Walker. Get ready to take your medicine."

"No. You wouldn't. Oh no, you—*Ah!* That's cold!"

The pale yellow liquid pooled exactly where he wanted it—in the small hollow of her throat. Lowering his head, he lapped at the ale until there was none, then pressed his tongue against her pounding pulse, feeling the fading vibration of her laughter.

And then there was only the sound of their rapid breathing, the call of migrating birds, the crunch of leaves as he settled himself firmly within the cradle of her thighs.

As quickly as the game had begun, it ceased. Raising up on his elbows, Grant looked down into her face, flushed from exertion, flushed with desire. There were leaves in her hair, and he stroked his fingers through the strands, plucking away each one.

She reached up and locked her hands around his neck, tracing the corded muscles there. He shivered, responding quickly to her light but evocative caress. When she pulled his head down to hers, he resisted only long enough to search her eyes.

Yes. The answer he craved was there.

Their mouths melded together. They rejoiced at the silent vow.

"Now?" he whispered, gliding his hand up her side, then cupping her breast. "Here? We don't have any—"

Shyly, she shook her head. "Tonight. I . . ." She looked away and whispered, "This sounds silly, but I wanted to wear my nightgown. It's always been a reminder and it seems only—"

"Perfect." He smiled, before his expression gave way to one of sensual need. "But in the meantime . . . I want to give you something to remember. Just to ensure you don't have a change of heart."

"I won't change my—"

Her breath caught. She exhaled his name on a trembling sigh as he pushed her breast upward. He kissed her through her shirt, wetting the fabric and puckering her nipple. The blood pulsed hotly through him, expanding his loins in anticipation.

"I've got a bottle of wine," he murmured, skimming his teeth back and forth, while his other hand fit beneath her buttocks and lifted her higher. "A cold front's blowing in, and there's plenty of wood for the fireplace."

He heard her small gasp and exulted in the signal of her escalating need as he rocked into her. Knowing what he did now, he was glad he had waited for her to initiate this. That he could do this to Cammie, that she could want him so much when she had never wanted anyone this way before . . . Oh, Lord, was there a happier man alive?

"Yes," she whispered. "Wine, a fire. I'd like that."

"As much as you like this?" Unable to withstand the temptation, and greedy to reassure himself he had the power to woo her body, he pushed up the old flannel shirt she wore, the one he'd outgrown by his thirteenth year.

She wasn't wearing a bra, and the wetness of the shirt had seeped over her areola. The wind whisked around her nipple and she moaned. He blew his warm breath onto her, then bent his head to toy, to kiss, to tease, and at last to open his mouth and take as much of her as he could.

She burrowed her hands deep into his hair, clasping him tight, tighter. She arched her back off the ground, seeking to bring him closer. As her hips strained upward, seeking his heat, he ground himself against her.

His body demanded immediate gratification; his mind rebelled against it. He had never been more frustrated, and yet, he was wonderfully satisfied that tonight would be perfect, unhindered by stray misgivings.

He laved each breast with his tongue while his hands worked the snap and zipper of her jeans. She raised her hips to help him, and he exulted in her lack of complacency, her eagerness to assist as he pushed her jeans aside.

"Just a taste," he murmured, pressing his lips against her stomach, the tip of his tongue dipping into the small, perfect navel. He rubbed his nose against her, inhaling her womanly scent.

"Grant," she whispered suddenly, and he could feel her stiffen. "Grant, I don't think—"

"Shhh. Don't think. Don't think at all, except about us. About how good this feels." Heedless of her small retreat, the faint pushing at his shoulders, he took his pleasure, certain that once she knew how good he made it for her, she would succumb.

And never refuse him again.

He sighed deeply with delight at the same time his breath quickened with the press of his lips into the haven of hers. She was moist in spite of her dwindling protests. As he probed and tasted and teased, he could hear her protests transform into muted moans, until her hands were no longer pushing, but pulling him deeper, closer.

He ached to forswear his patience, to strip right there and pump his body into hers until they were too exhausted to do more than cry their release. But it wouldn't work that way. He could hurt her and destroy this newfound bond that even now he strengthened. And even now he did what he could to make her more ready, to prepare her body and, he hoped, lessen the hurt.

His fingers sought her, learned her, and skillfully stretched until she was no longer moist, but ecstatically *wet.*

"Please," she suddenly cried. "Please, Grant. I *need* you . . . *now.*"

Her body began to tremble, and he gave her what he could. Though what he gave wasn't nearly enough, it sufficed.

"It—it happened," she whispered with awe. "Oh, Lord, thank you. I prayed so many times, but I never dreamed . . . never . . ."

"Oh, Cammie. You don't know how good it *will* be. This was only a taste, a tiny taste," he whispered against her ear, lapping at the tears trekking downward. "Tonight, we'll feast together."

"Yes, yes." She sobbed, not completely fulfilled, yet in wonder at the ecstasy she was feeling. "Tonight. Together at last."

Grant stirred the fire, glad the cold front had given them the excuse to build it. He'd even mulled the burgundy wine. Dinner was over, but the candles still burned.

He'd showered, shaved, put on a fresh set of clothes. He'd never married, having hung on to illusions that had now miraculously come true. A proposal was in the making and a honeymoon imminent.

"Grant?"

Savoring the anticipation, he put aside the bellows, then turned. What he saw was a vision. A woman in silk scarlet and out of a dream he'd replayed too many times to count. It gave him a sense of déjà vu.

"Are you real?" he asked, his voice almost cracking with urgency, with too many years of anticipation. "Or am I going to wake up and discover this really was too good to be true?"

Panic surged within Cammie, tempting her to delay. Turning her back to the old ghosts, she walked bravely forward, not stopping until she was less than an arm's length away. She notched her chin higher, internally challenging the demons.

"Why don't you touch me and see?" she asked. The words hadn't come easily, but still she had said them and was proud for that.

Grant held his hand over her right breast, not touching, but hovering close enough for her to feel the heat, feel her breast tauten and strain toward him.

"Once I touch you," he said, "I won't be able to stop. I want to feel you, I want to taste you, and I want to hear you cry out my name. It's driving me mad; I've needed you for so long. I want to make sure you realize that from here, there's no turning back. Tell me you understand that."

She swallowed hard. "I understand."

"And you want me too."

In answer, she stepped forward, bringing his palm flush against her breast. She covered his hand with hers and pressed. Her flesh seemed to burn through the silk, hotter than the fire crackling in the hearth.

She heard his indrawn breath, matching hers. His eyes narrowed, while his features blended into a mixture of self-control, limitless love, and a rapacious hunger that was frightening in its intensity.

"Touch me," he commanded in a hoarse voice. "Anywhere. Everywhere. Just do it and don't ever stop."

The second her fingers began to work the buttons of his shirt, he slipped a thumb beneath each lacy strap and nudged the gown off her shoulders.

"I want to touch you," she said. She pushed aside his shirt, but hesitated at his belt. "It's still . . . not easy. Even when I want you as much as I do now."

"Practice," he murmured wisely, while shifting the fitted bodice down to her waist. "It'll never become easy unless you do. And besides, you're doing a wonderful job. No woman's ever had this kind of hold over me, Cammie. Just looking at you half-dressed is more arousing than any act of sex I've ever indulged in."

"Then at least I'm not the only one," she said, peeking from beneath lowered lashes. Wanting no secrets, she rushed on. "I have a confession to make, Grant. I—I saw you that night, climbing out of the hot tub. I ran away, but not before it was too late. I wanted you then. It appalled me, but I couldn't help myself."

"Thank God," he said, then added with a chuckle, "When we get back, I think I'll have that hot tub enshrined."

"I don't think you were alone that night. You were . . . aroused."

He furrowed his brow, remembering. "No . . . No, I wasn't alone. But it was because I couldn't have you that I went to someone else."

"I hated her," Cammie confessed quietly. "I hated her for having you when I couldn't."

"Jealous, were you?" he prompted with a satisfied smile.

"Insanely." Encouraged, she reached for his belt with shaking hands. "There have been . . . a lot of women in your life, haven't there?"

"Too many. And all the wrong ones." He guided her hands to shed the last of his clothes. The makeshift bed of blankets on the floor welcomed them as Grant led her down. "Only you were the right one. They simply helped numb the void. Without you, Cammie, I'm empty inside." He leaned over her, cradling her face between his hands. "*Fill me,*" he whispered urgently, "while I fill you."

"Yes. Oh, *yes,*" she said, and reached for him, suddenly more afraid of the emptiness without him than she had ever been of taking his forbidden offering. Nothing existed except the awful need, except the two of them and the craving to become one.

Work—gone. Parents—gone. The future could take care of itself. Nothing mattered but this man she loved more than any person alive or dead; this man, whose masterful hands helped her thrust the last of her fears into oblivion.

As he touched her intimately, plied her flesh with loving, agile fingers, with his clever mouth and tongue, she thrashed against the silk nightgown, its encumbrance unforgivable for keeping even a fraction of their bodies apart.

Finally, naked, entwined, they sought the secrets of each other's skin, nothing hidden or left untouched. She stroked him as he caressed her, marveling in the length and breadth of his body, delighting in his whispers of encouragement and groans of delight.

How long they wrestled and fondled, she didn't

know. She only knew that if he didn't take her at last, she would go mad.

"Don't wait," she pleaded through kiss-swollen lips. "If you wait, I'll die."

"We'll die again and again," he promised, his teeth clenched with the effort of restraint. "We'll die the little death together when I bury myself inside you . . . when we're finally one."

Quickly, he sheathed himself. She regretted even that between them, and told him so.

"I hate it too," he whispered roughly. "Because I want it all. I want you to feel me hot and surging, coming inside as deep as I can reach."

"Reach now," she begged. "Don't stop until you're home." Shamelessly, beyond caring, she spread her legs and guided him to the threshold of her virginity, knowing there would be pain, but none that could rival the agony of his absence.

Sliding his hand between their bodies, he stimulated her with slow, sensitive caresses, while he eased himself inside, just the smallest bit. She arched up for more, but he held back. She panted his name and quivered, while he whispered sex words, love words, to stoke her spiraling hunger.

Would he never appease her? she wondered dazedly. Was it some kind of torture he was bent on administering? With a growl that was animalistic, so primal it surely hadn't come from her, she sank her nails into his back and was rewarded with an answering, hoarse groan.

"You want me. You need me."

"Yes, yes," she chanted. "More than anything, yes."

"And you're in love with me."

"I do love you, Grant. You know I do."

"Say you're *in* love with me. Forever in love."

"I'm *in love with you, Grant.* Madly, passionately. Yes, forev—"

The words caught as he thrust into her. He sealed his mouth over hers, swallowing her sharp cry as if it were his own. The emptiness was suddenly too full, and her body jerked in protest.

"Easy, easy," he whispered. "Hold tight to me, and I promise to make it right."

He soothed her, held her captive with his weight, with his kisses, until her body miraculously adjusted to make a perfect fit. Then he began to move with slow, expert strokes. Gradually, when she was sure this was only becoming better, the pain a wondrous precursor to ecstasy, she began to move slightly with him.

Grant murmured his praise and increased her pleasure. When she thought it could never be better, it suddenly was. He was entering her fast and deep, and she was rising, endlessly rising to greet each powerful thrust, riding with him on a tidal wave that cast them both higher, far from reality.

She looked up into his face, and saw his eyes were slitted with passion, every muscle strained, taut. There was the smell of fire, of musk, of sweat . . . and then her world broke apart, flinging her in so many directions that she thought she must have died and this was paradise. She called to him and he joined her, pulsing with life, with love, and, as they rocked complete in each other's arms, with the joy of ecstasy's laughter.

Somehow they made it to the bedroom with the wine. He hadn't carried her—they had remained mated each step of the way. Their endless coupling was a ballet of epic proportions. Tender, ravenous, sensual, erotic, a hedonistic indulgence of the senses that must have been blessed by heaven but was so marvelously, deliciously wanton, it had to be sin.

The wine was long gone, and so were her inhibitions. They had no secrets left, and there was no room for regrets.

Gazing at his sleeping form, Cammie offered a prayer of thanks. Her heart overflowed at the sight of him, the beauty that was Grant. He was a modern-day Adonis, externally more beautiful than any man had a right to be. But that wasn't his real allure. It was *him*. What he was inside, which far exceeded the outside package.

His parents were exceptional people. They had to be to have given birth to and raised such a man.

Cammie sighed and her brows drew together. It was the first time she'd let herself think about them, about the issue that remained unresolved between her and Grant.

They had two more days together to discuss what they should do. She didn't want to taint the wonder of the night by concerns that wouldn't go away, but could wait. Just as she thought she and Grant should wait, make sure this was forever, before risking the family balance.

Snuggling deeper into his embrace, she pushed the unwanted thoughts aside and pressed a kiss against his neck. Before she could whisper "Good morning," he rolled her onto her back, holding her hands high above her head.

"For being in such a deep sleep," she said, "you sure are a quick riser." She giggled as his beard scratched her chin, then he lowered to nuzzle a plump, ivory breast.

He nudged her hips with his and growled, "I rise a lot quicker than you think, young lady."

She gasped as he thrust inside her and then lay very still.

"Is that safe?" she asked, noticing she was sore but most definitely accommodating. He fit tight, perfect, secure.

"Not too smart probably, but for a minute, I think we're safe. Be still, don't move. Just let me feel myself inside before I wake up and have to act rationally."

"I don't want to act rationally," she whispered impulsively. "I want us to make love again and again and never stop."

"For a lifetime and more," he concurred. His eyes bored into hers, serious eyes that matched a serious voice. "Cammie Walker, I want you always. In the good times and the bad. I want to—"

They both stiffened at the sound of a car pulling up close to the cottage. Within moments there followed a loud *thud* of a shutting door. For a split second they stared wordlessly at each other.

Familiar voices outside had Grant rolling off her, automatically reaching for a nonexistent pair of jeans. Cammie sprang off the bed, frantically scrambling for a robe when all she could find was the discarded wine bottle. Her scarlet nightie lay in a heap with Grant's clothes in front of the fireplace.

"What are we going to do, Grant?" she asked urgently.

He was already headed for the small living room, and in seconds flat was throwing on his pants. The red nightgown sailed in her direction just as she heard a knock on the front door.

Grant tossed the discarded blankets into her room, then leaned in as his gaze traced her nude body, which was shaking, and not from the cold.

"You get dressed," he said calmly. "I'll make

coffee for Mom and Dad, and get them ready to hear the news."

"What?" she croaked, fumbling around for anything besides the incriminating gown to wear. "What news?"

"Why, about *us*, of course."

Eleven

"No!" She shook her head emphatically while she scrambled through a drawer. She jumped into a pair of sweatpants so fast, he thought her life must have depended on it. "Grant, *no*. It's too soon."

He heard the jangle of a key being fit into the lock, but chose to ignore it. Cammie's opposition was far more disturbing than being discovered.

"What do you *mean* it's too soon? There'll never be a good time, Cammie. The sooner we set the record straight, the better."

"Not yet! Grant, please. I'm begging you—"

"Knock, knock," Edward called. "Anybody home?"

Cammie's pleading eyes were the last thing Grant saw before she lunged forward and shut the bedroom door.

His heart sank, an iciness wrapping around it at her rejection. Oh, how he hurt. It was too deep, too deep.

Drawing on more self-control than he knew he

possessed, he forbade himself to kick open the door and drag her out half-dressed to confront the final obstacle.

He turned, his mouth set in a grim line—the closest he could get to a smile—just as his parents entered the cottage.

"Well, if you don't look a mess," his mother chided as she scanned the untidy room. "Looks like y'all had a party and forgot to invite us along. Really, Grant. Sleeping till noon? You and Cammie must have been enjoying yourselves last night."

"Oh, yeah," he said as raw emotions twisted through his gut. "We had a ball." Rapping sharply on Cammie's door, he called, "Hey, Cammie, wake up. The folks are here. They want to hear all about the good time we had last night."

With a jovial laugh, his father added, "Next vacation, we'll join you. Guess we got here late, but better late than never, right, Dotty?"

The door behind Grant cracked open and Cammie peeked out, her face pale and anxious.

"Hi, Mom and Dad. Guess we slept late. As soon as I'm dressed, I'll meet you in the kitchen."

"Cammie," Dorothy said with maternal alarm, "you look ten times worse than Grant. You're not ill, are you?"

Before Cammie could retreat, Dorothy hurried forward to put a hand against her forehead.

"No fever," she concluded, clucking her tongue while Cammie began to look even worse.

"No, no, I'm just tired," she muttered, glancing nervously at Grant. "I'll be fine as soon as I take a shower and drink a cup of coffee."

Grant glared accusingly at her, and she quickly dropped her gaze.

"I'll fix you kids something to eat," Dorothy said, and headed for the kitchen. "I do declare, children.

We leave you alone for a week and you wear yourselves out. Is that any way to spend your vacation?"

"We wouldn't have spent it any other way, would we, Cammie?" Grant said.

"No," she said in a faint voice that made him want to shake her.

"So how many fish did you catch so far, son?" Edward asked as he and Grant followed Dorothy. "Did Cammie beat you as usual?"

"We're tied for once," he said shortly, stealing a last glance at Cammie and hating the silent plea he read in her eyes. "I think her luck just ran out. Because this time I mean to win."

Grant stared straight ahead at the road, the silence in the car thick and stretching as far as the blur of yellow lines on the highway. He glanced over at Cammie, who was concentrating too hard on the needlework in her lap.

In a fit of frustration he snatched the embroidery hoop out of her hands and hurled it into the minuscule backseat.

"They're gone," he said curtly. "You can drop the 'all's well' routine. As we both know, all is *not* well. That farce we put up is still turning my stomach."

"I can't believe they came to keep us company." Cammie gripped her own middle as though she were the one battling illness. "It was like a dream turning into a nightmare. Hearing them outside when we were . . ." She shuddered.

"Finish the sentence, Cammie," he challenged hotly.

"Please, Grant. I'm not up to fighting with you about this. I'm still shaking from the ordeal."

"Okay, then *I'll* finish it," he snapped. "Hearing

them outside when we were having sex. Hot, don't ever stop, make love to me forever, sex." But he wouldn't mention, he added silently, that he was about to ask her to marry him, to sleep in his bed every night and have his babies. Or that he was even ready to make a fool of himself and start spouting poetry. "Come, grow old with me, the best is yet to be . . ." Hah!

"Why do you have to be so nasty about it, Grant? Can't you let it drop until we can discuss this rationally?"

"No, I can't. And believe me, I'm not being half as nasty as I'd like. Thanks to you, we're still Mom and Dad's little angels, not two adults in charge of our own lives who don't need parental consent to make our own decisions."

"Being adult means acting responsibly," she countered. "You certainly weren't doing your share, brooding and sulking and making a bad situation even worse. Mom asked us what was wrong so many times, I lost count."

"I'll tell you what's wrong. In my book, being responsible means owning up to your convictions and being honest, especially with the people you love. We owe them that. We owe *ourselves* that. Not a mouthful of lies."

"Oh?" she retorted angrily. "We owed it to them to leave the condom wrapper on the floor since they didn't luck out and find us rolling around naked?"

Grant's jaw clenched tight as he remembered the discarded wrapper lying in clear sight, and Cammie almost breaking her neck to step on it before anyone saw.

"If you moved half as fast at confessing the truth as you did trying to cover it up," he said, "the worst would be over with and we could all get on with our lives. I don't like subterfuge. It goes against my grain." He shot her a censuring glare. "But apparently not yours."

"That's not true! I'm simply trying to keep from hurting innocent people."

"So you hurt us instead. How charitable of you, Cammie."

Her injured expression told him he'd hit his mark.

"How can you be so hateful after what we shared?" she asked.

"How can *you* act so ashamed of us being in love, of showing it the way we're meant to? You think they don't know what it means to commit? To show it by sharing their bodies? For heaven's sake, they're crazy about each other. They gave birth to two children. If anyone could understand, it should be Mom and Dad."

He snorted in disgust and deliberately threw down the gauntlet. "I swear, Cammie, didn't you learn anything from living with them? Wake up and grow up. Start acting like a grown woman instead of a kid who got caught playing doctor."

"You—you—Damn you, Grant. If you weren't driving this car right now I'd hit you for—What are you doing?"

Grant stopped the Porsche on a dime, squealing to a halt on the side of the road so suddenly that they were both jerked forward.

Facing her squarely, he offered his cheek. "I'm not driving. Go ahead, Cammie. Hit me. Make it good, because I could use some honest pain. The kind that shows. Not the kind that's turning me inside out because you won't admit to them you're in love with me. The way you've been the last two days, I don't know if you're so sure about it yourself."

"I am!" The eyes that seconds before had snapped fire now shone with hurt that he could doubt her. "I *am* in love with you, Grant. It's just that we need more time. We have to know where we're headed, that this is for good, before we do something irreversible that affects a lot more lives than our own."

"Why wait?" He hit the dashboard in exasperation. "What kind of odds are you looking for?"

"I want us to be sure." She reached for his hand, and he could have cursed the power she held to make him weak with longing. "I want us to spend time together like every couple does before they . . ." Her voice trailed off.

"Get married?" At last, he thought. Out in the open where it should have been all along.

Cammie hesitated, then nodded. "Yes, I suppose that's what we're talking about."

"You suppose. Damn, Cammie, can't you even bring yourself to say it?"

"All right!" she snapped. "Marriage. The *M* word. The thing we both know I'm so good at making plans for but never going through with. Let's face it, Grant. My track record's nothing to brag about."

"How soon you forget," he said smoothly, deciding to catch her off guard in hopes it would net the results he wanted. Clasping her upper arms, he leaned close to her and brushed his chest across her breasts, while his mouth hovered a whisper's distance away. Her eyes widened, and he could feel her nipples immediately tauten. Nearly two days had passed since he'd held her, and the hunger eating at him likely had something to do with his short fuse.

"If you remember," he continued, "we broke all sorts of your previous records in the last week.

Don't give me that excuse again, and don't ever make the mistake of putting me in the same category as your other men."

"I never said you were like them," she whispered breathlessly, her gaze lingering on his mouth. "You're nothing like any other man I've known."

"That's right, Cammie. And if you want to lay odds on us working out, I suggest you consider this: The very things you say are working against us, are exactly what we have going in our favor."

"Our family? You're presuming a lot, Grant."

"I don't think so. We've got a long history together. We're incredibly compatible when we're not at each other's throats. We genuinely love each other, without any of the false illusions most couples have. And as for physical attraction . . ." He traced her lips with his tongue while he flicked a fingertip across her breast. She moaned in a most gratifying way. "Let's just say it's intense."

"Grant," she whispered, clasping his shoulders, seeking his mouth.

He pulled back before he lost sight of his purpose.

"Not so fast. I want to turn around and take care of business the way we should have two days ago."

She abruptly drew away, the smoldering desire banked just as quickly as he'd inflamed it.

"No, Grant," she said firmly. "In time. But not just yet."

With a curse, he threw the car back into gear and peeled out. His brows drawn into a heavy frown, he aimed his bitter disappointment like an accusing arrow and hit the bull's-eye with a poignant sting.

"That shrink owes you a refund, Cammie, for a misdiagnosis. Your problem isn't just loss, or that you can't commit to a man. It's that you can't make a commitment to yourself."

"Wait, Cammie! Jeez, would you just hold on a minute and tell me what's eating you?"

"Move," she growled, hoisting her bag out of the trunk with adrenaline-fired strength. She pushed past Grant to the front door, ready to slam it shut in his face; only he was quicker and slammed it open again.

"All right. That's it! Spit it out, Cammie, let me have it."

"I don't want to talk to you," she said through pinched lips. "I, for one, prefer to talk when I'm not itching to do bodily harm to some *jerk* who betrays my confidence."

"Ah-hah! Now we're getting somewhere."

She spun on her heel, silently seething. At least if she seethed, she thought, she could blank out the hurt, the wound that Grant had inflicted with such callous indifference.

"We're not getting anywhere," she said shortly. "You're going home, out of my sight, before I do something rash."

"Dammit, Cammie. Come here—*agh!*" He grabbed his right knee, where he'd knocked his old football injury against the edge of her couch. Hobbling as fast as he could, he went after her.

The bedroom door slammed shut, followed by the sound of a *click*.

Banging on the wood, he bellowed, "Let me in. Do you hear me, Cammie Walker? I demand that you unlock this door, right this instant."

"Go away. I don't want to see your traitor's face, Grant Kennedy. Just go away and leave me alone."

"Either you let me in or I'm knocking this door flat. Cammie! Cammie, did you hear me?"

She buried her head under the pillow to muffle the sobs she'd held back for the last hour, ignoring his threat and the persistent banging.

Once he'd quit pounding on the door, she threw the pillow against it, pretending it was his handsome face—the face she itched to slap at the moment.

Just as the pillow hit the mark, a loud crash accompanied the sound of splintering wood. The door flew back on groaning hinges, revealing Grant, his expression livid and pained as he rubbed his upper arm.

"Now look what you did!" she yelled, impatiently dashing away her tears. "You broke my door."

"So send me the bill." He stalked to the edge of the bed and yanked her upright, his face inches from hers. "If you've got a problem or a bone to pick with me, I want to hear it straight to my face. But don't you *ever* lock me out again, do you understand?"

"I'll tell you what I understand." She tried to fling his hands away, but he only tightened his grip. Stung into retaliation, she hurled her accusation with righteous wrath.

"I had a problem—a problem that was so deep, I couldn't stand to face it myself. I trusted you with a sensitive part of my life, Grant, something that no one else will ever see. And what did you do? You took that confidence, my trust, and turned it against me."

"I *what*?" His scowl disappeared, replaced by an expression of puzzlement and concern.

"You heard me. It was so important to you to be right, you didn't care how deep you twisted the knife to make your point. 'It's not that you can't make a commitment to a man. Your problem is, you can't make a commitment to yourself.' That's what you said, and I don't think I'll ever forget it. Right now, I can't forgive it, either, so don't waste your breath apologizing."

"I'm not apologizing, because it was the truth," he insisted bullishly. "I was trying to make you face up to what's really keeping us apart."

"Is it the truth? Maybe to your one-track mind it is, since the only right way to do anything is your way. But in my book, I *have* made commitments—big ones."

"Name them."

"All right. First—" She tried to hold up a finger, but he locked her hand against him, her arms pinned to his chest. It made her even madder, at him, at herself, because despite her rage, the contact thrilled her. "While you've had years to adjust to the idea of 'us,' I've had barely a month. It was a tremendous leap on my part to accept that, to give 'us' a chance."

His brow furrowed as he considered the point. At the moment she found his penchant for analyzing everything grating, irritating. She could practically see the wheels turning as he examined her statement for validity and flaws.

"Okay," he finally conceded. "That does have some merit. But what else, Cammie? What have you done to give 'us' a chance? What commitments have you made to the relationship? *That's* what I want to know."

She stared at him, mouth agape. "For being such a genius, you must be the most obtuse man I've ever met."

He smiled slowly, indulgently. "A few days ago you told me I was the most patient, the most wonderful—"

"Don't you dare trivialize this," she spat, not believing he had the audacity to smile in the face of her hurt, her fury. "Two days ago I went to bed with you. I gave you my virginity and shared something no other man has ever come close to. *I bared my soul.* We were as intimate as a man and woman can possibly get, and you *dare* to accuse me of not making a commitment to us, to myself."

"Cammie, I—"

"Just shut up, Grant. Shut the hell—" Her voice broke, and she could feel tears gather. The horrible intrusion on their lovemaking, the strain, their fighting, all culminated in a sob she detested but couldn't control.

"I hate you," she cried, wresting her arm free and striking his chest. "Do you hear me? I hate you. I gave you access to the deepest part of me and you turned it against me to get your way. I made commitments, I—I said and did things that were hard for me. I did it for *us*. And just when I was feeling good about myself, about coming so far, you ruin it. You belittled me, Grant. And for that, I hate you. I—I hate . . ."

She began to weep. She pummeled his chest while he held her, making no effort to stop the blows. She struck him until she had no strength left, and when she would have slumped, he gathered her into his arms.

"You love me," he whispered into her hair. "You love me. Even when you hate me, you love me." He stroked his fingers through the tangle of curls, pressed his lips against her temple, then lapped gently at the tears.

He guided her down onto the bed and kissed her. Her face, her throat, and finally her mouth. The taste of salt and violent emotion was between them, and she fought the urge to forget her words, their differences, and simply give in. It would be so easy . . . and so wrong.

"No," she whispered. "No. Leave me alone."

"Never," he murmured, and straddled her thighs, settling his hips in the cradle of hers.

In a last-ditch effort to maintain her own sense of rightness, she tried to thrust him away. He used his superior strength and clasped her wrists with a single hand, tying them both to the bond that could never be denied.

"Not like this," she whimpered. "It's not right. Not with our fighting, not with this between us."

He held her still with the power of his gaze, deep and full of regret.

"I'm sorry," he said. "I'm sorry for hurting you. But I was hurting so much myself, I lashed out. Forgive me for that, because I only want us both to be happy. Tell me what you need, Cammie. Just tell me."

"Time," she whispered.

"How much?"

"I—I don't know."

"A week, a month? Tell me how much, and let's work it out."

She didn't know, she honestly didn't. This wasn't like the countdown before the camera began to roll. A week wouldn't do it; neither would a month . . .

"Three months, Grant. Give us three months and we'll see how far we've come."

"That's a long—"

"If you believe in us, it'll work out, no matter how much time it takes."

His mouth covered hers, and his tongue swirled against, around, and parried with hers. She responded, and as he released her wrists she wrapped her arms about his neck. Her pride insisted she shouldn't give in, yet in her heart she knew it had never been more right.

"Three months," he agreed, then sealed it with a heart-stopping kiss. He cradled her face between his palms, his eyes revealing naked, emotional need. "I hate it when we argue. Tell me you forgive me."

"I forgive you."

"Tell me you love me."

"I . . . love you." And she did, so much that she hurt. She loved him in spite of his maddening nature, just as she loved him because of it.

He led her hand down to his groin.

"Show me. Touch me. I need you." His hand glided up her inner thigh, then he unfastened her jeans. Tugging the zipper down, he whispered, "I want to undo the damage. I need to know I can still make you need me."

She needed to know too. She needed the reassurance that the ground she'd gained was intact, challenged but stronger for it.

Her anger spent, the hurt diminishing fast and supplanted by passion, she unzipped his pants and grasped him in her hand.

He was hard. Pulsing. For her, only for her.

"You're wet," he murmured, relief and victory suffusing his discovery.

A pearly drop of his liquid answered hers, life unborn, yet symbolic of one that could be theirs together.

With a cry, she rejoiced in their mutual need, their undaunted love. Their lovemaking was frantic, urgent to forgive.

It was a pact sealed in flesh, a commitment to believe in tomorrow.

Twelve

"Cammie, sweetheart, would you go ask Grant how long before the turkey's done? He's had it on the grill all mornin', so surely it's about ready."

"Sure, Mom. Want me to help set the table after that?"

"You always love settin' that good china of Grandma's out, don't you?"

"You bet, Thanksgiving only comes once a year."

"Thank goodness," chimed in Trish. "All this dishwashing by hand and football games ad nauseam is once a year too many, if you ask me."

Cammie slid Trish a sidelong glance that silently agreed. She could do without the dishwashing, too, and fancy china wasn't at the top of her list of priorities. But she knew how much Dorothy enjoyed using it, and she, too, liked what it symbolized. Knowing it had belonged to Grant's grandmother gave her a sense of posterity and kinship. The handing down from generation to generation was something she equated with security—like Grant.

Glad for the excuse to seek him out, she set the bowl of fruit salad she'd just finished making into the refrigerator.

"Don't take too long," Trish whispered with a knowing wink, "or I'll have to cover for you again."

"Thanks, Trish," she muttered under her breath before heading to the back porch, where Grant was basting the turkey.

Nothing had been admitted, nothing had been asked, yet Trish had left little doubt that she was on to them—and approved. Thank heaven for Trish, Cammie thought. Though she still shuddered to think of how their parents might react, it was wonderfully reassuring to know Trish would be in their corner when the lid blew.

Six weeks down, six to go to judgment day. She dreaded it. She was also weary of the farce. Grant was chomping at the bit, but he was making a valiant effort to give her time. He slipped occasionally, pressuring her. And the episodes were on the rise. But he had her number, always managing to turn a battlefield into a negotiation that ended in passion.

He was bent over the turkey, basting it with his usual level of concentration, she noticed. She longed to go to him, to slip her arms around his waist and rest her cheek against his broad, strong back.

"Hey, Bro," she said instead. "Are you about done with that, or do we have to wait till Christmas?"

Grant turned at the sound of her voice. The nickname no longer irritated him. It had become a joke of sorts, and he was glad they had come far enough to laugh about things that hadn't been funny in the past. Progress. Yes, they were moving ever forward. Only not fast enough to suit him.

"I figured if I stayed out here long enough," he said, "they'd send you to check on me. Just another reason why we need to fess up, babe—so they could eat on time. Not to mention you could mosey on over here and plant one on me right this minute, instead of standing there looking hungry." He gave her a leering grin. "And we both know I'm not talking turkey."

"You're incorrigible." She smiled, then wet her lips in a deliberately seductive gesture.

"If you like living on the edge, just keep that up."

To taunt him, she slowly repeated the action, then giggled. "I'll keep it up."

"Okay, that does it. You've pushed me too far this time."

"Grant!" she yelped as he quickly strode over to her and hoisted her over his shoulder. "What do you think you're doing? Someone could come out here any minute!"

She kicked her feet and he gave her a swat on the behind.

"Keep up the ruckus, Sis, and we'll have an audience for sure."

He rounded the corner to the side of the house, glanced around to make sure they were alone, then slowly slid her down his length and pressed her back against the wood. All play ceased, and they seized the stolen moment of privacy. His lips found hers, quick, sure, proprietary. He hated the subterfuge, just as he craved the haven of her mouth, the familiar warmth of her body molding into a natural fit against his.

"Ahem."

Cammie pushed him away, distress immediately surfacing on her flushed face, marring the glow of desire. Oh, how he hated it, resented her retreat.

He was slow to release her, but faced their

intruder with an expression of challenge, and pleasure. To be seen together, openly, the way it was meant to be. Yes, he delighted in that.

Heedless of her furtive struggles, he embraced Cammie with a firm arm beneath her breasts, pulling her intimately against him, her back to his chest.

"Hello, Trish," he said in a lazy, nonchalant tone. He hoped Cammie would take the cue to relax, find her own ease with the openness he felt. "What brings you here?"

"Just thought I'd check on the status of . . . what's cookin'"—she chuckled—"before Mom could beat me to it."

"What's cookin' is *us*, as apparently you've already guessed."

"I'll say. Some of those looks you've been exchanging lately could torch Antartica. I'm horribly jealous, of course. Seeing you together makes me realize how much I miss Mark."

"You don't think Mom and Dad know, do you?" Cammie's voice was anxious. Grant stifled an angry curse.

Trish looked from one to the other, then shrugged. "I don't think so. They're pretty near-sighted when it comes to us, as we all know."

Grant could feel the sigh of relief leave Cammie's chest, and he tightened his hold in reflexive frustration.

"Cammie and I are serious, Trish," he said.

"So I gathered."

"But we don't see eye to eye about how the folks might take the news."

"Grant, would you quit trying to drag Trish into our dispute? This is between us and not—"

"Hey, she's family," he argued. "I thought we should get an objective perspective."

"I don't think—"

"Look, y'all," Trish interrupted, "I'm bowing out. Cammie's right. This is between the two of you. I don't know how Mom and Dad might react, but as for me, I'm for you one hundred percent." She gave them a considering look and added, "Anybody ever tell you what a cute couple you make? You look good together."

"We *are* good together." Grant pressed his palm flat against Cammie's abdomen and kissed her temple. "Aren't we, Cammie?"

"Yes, Grant," she said, loud enough for Trish to hear, which was the most encouraging sign he'd had yet. That and her impulsive kiss on his hand. "And we're good *for* each other."

Her stiffness had gradually yielded to softness. She leaned against him naturally. The way it should be, he thought, proud to be seen together. Recognized as the inseparable, match-made-in-heaven couple they were. Trish's discovering them had validated them somehow—and it only made him yearn for more. A ring, an altar, a church full of witnesses.

Unexpectedly, Trish dabbed at her eyes, then stepped forward to put her arms around them both.

"I love y'all so much. You've always been there, in the best of times. And the worst. And it makes me so happy to see you this way. It shows on your faces, makes me remember how much I miss—" Her voice caught. "Ah, hell, I'm such a sap for a love story. Just be good to each other. Don't ever take what you've got for granted, 'cause one day it's there and the next it's gone." She dashed aside a runaway tear, then summoned a jaunty smile. "Okay, while you finish swapping some spit, I'll tell everyone the turkey's on it's way."

As soon as Trish rounded the corner, Grant turned Cammie to him.

"She still misses him," she said sadly.

"Would you miss me as much?"

"At least."

He regarded her a moment, his head tilted in thought. "Given that, dare I hope you're coming around?"

"Time, Grant. But I'm getting there."

"I know. That's the first time you've kissed me in front of someone. And it felt good, Cammie. For me it was something I needed. Did it mean nearly as much to you?"

"Yes," she confessed. "It was good not to hide for a change. It felt . . . almost natural after a little while."

"That's what I wanted to hear. Life's too precious, Cammie. And Trish is right: We should make each minute count." He pulled her close and pressed his lips to her forehead. "Know what I'm giving thanks for today?"

"The same thing I am?"

He smiled. "Depends on what that is."

"Do you even have to ask?" Wrapping her arms tight about his neck, she urged his mouth to hers.

"Go ahead, open it."

"I want to guess first." Cammie shook the elaborately wrapped gold and silver box. "Now let me see . . . Could it be a new dorm shirt? The one you gave me a few years back is getting a little ratty."

He chuckled. "Fat chance. I'd rather see you in nothing than that. Of course, a few years ago that was the closest I could get to sleeping with you."

"Little did I guess."

"And if you'd known?"

She cocked her head, thinking back. "I would have been shocked."

"Offended?"

"I don't think so . . . but then again, I wouldn't have been ready for this." She reached for Grant's hand and kissed it, close to his ring finger.

A wedding ring would be there by now, he thought, if he could have his way. Clamping down on the never-ceasing urge to propose, he settled for testing the waters.

"*Are* you ready, Cammie? We could see the new year in together without sneaking off alone like we are tonight. I think the folks are pretty disappointed we're getting in so late for Christmas Eve."

The careful tearing of the foil wrap suddenly ceased. Cammie bit her lower lip.

"Grant, please. Let's not spoil Christmas Eve by beating a dead horse. This is a special time, and it's up to us to talk to your parents when we won't upset their holidays. That would be really selfish on our part."

"So you do admit we are going to talk to them."

"It's . . . inevitable. Eventually."

He snorted his disgust. "At the rate we're going, they'll get the news at the pearly gates. I gotta tell you, Cammie, all this pretense over the holidays is taking its toll. I won't go through this again next year."

"Next year . . ." She sighed. "I'm sure by next year we'll have everything worked out."

"Meaning?"

"Meaning I'm in love with you, Grant. And I know things are coming to a head. But it's Christmas Eve and we've only got three hours until we have to be at the folks', and we aren't going to solve our problems before then. I want to make what little time we've got left count. Now let me open my present so I can give you yours."

The only present he wanted was her acceptance to a proposal of marriage. While she returned to unwrapping the package, he tried not to think of the ring in his pocket, the real gift he longed to offer, to slip on her finger and seal with a vow of love.

The black satin-and-lace teddy spilled out, followed by a pair of heart-shaped diamond studs. They were meant to match the locket and the hairpins she wore on the news each night. A lover's gift, a husband's gift, suitable to wear down the aisle.

"Oh, Grant," she breathed. "They're gorgeous . . . and outrageously extravagant. You're spoiling me rotten, and—"

"And you can come here to thank me properly."

He reached for her, and she went eagerly into his arms, feathering kisses over his face.

"You didn't say anything about the lingerie," he said.

"It's beautiful. But where did you find something so . . . decadent? It's sexy as sin."

"Like you, babe. I want you to wear it tonight."

"You mean you want me to try it on now?"

"No. Tonight. When everyone's asleep and you sneak into my room. Trish won't care if she sleeps by herself."

"You've got to be kidding."

"I'm dead serious. We've slept together every night for over a month. I have no intention to start sleeping by myself on Christmas Eve."

Cammie drew back, firmly shaking her head. The teddy slipped from her hands and onto the floor, but she didn't seem to notice. Grant picked it up and nuzzled his nose in it.

"I also intend to get this close. I want you in my bed—the one I spent years alone in, dreaming you were with me. It's important to me, Cammie. Tonight. *That* bed. *That* house. It means more, something no other place can touch. If you can't bring yourself to say what needs to be said, at least give me that much of a commitment. Show me you want me, even there. *Especially* there."

Still she shook her head. "Grant, it's too risky. I want to sleep with you too. But what you want isn't right. Someone could hear. Or walk in. Or we could fall asleep and they'd discover us—No. I still can't forget what happened at the cottage. This could prove even worse."

"We'll be quiet. No one comes in my room when the door's locked. I'll set the alarm to go off before anyone else is up." He pressed his lips against her neck, then nibbled on her earlobe. "You're out of excuses, Cammie. Take your pick. It's them or me tonight. I need to know who's more important. Like I said a long time ago, I want it all. And your loyalty is part of the package."

The delighted smile of a few minutes before was replaced by an expression of painful uncertainty. Grant tightened his lips as his frustration escalated. What she was giving wasn't enough. He wanted, needed, craved more. What he'd just demanded was a test; he had to know where he stood.

"Open your present," she urged, sidestepping the commitment he was pushing for as she extricated herself from his grip. She picked up a small package from beneath the tree they had decorated together, and extended it to him. He looked from the box to her.

"That's a pretty poor substitute, don't you think?"

"How do you know? You haven't opened it yet."

Gritting his teeth with what little he had left of the Christmas spirit, Grant tore open the wrapping. His frown transformed into a smile.

"Grant and Cammie," he read from the engraving on the back of the thin gold watch, "Forever in Time."

"Like it?" she asked anxiously.

"I love it. But not as much as I love you."

They embraced, and for the moment what they had was almost enough.

"Good night, Mom. Good night, Dad. Good night, Grant. Merry Christmas."

"'Night, Cammie," Dorothy and Edward echoed. "'Night, Trish. Good night, Grant. See you all on Christmas morning."

Trish bid everyone a pleasant sleep before climbing into bed and saying, "Hey, Cammie. Is it just me, or does this sound like an old rerun of *The Waltons*?"

"I always liked *The Waltons*," Cammie answered with a sad smile. In so many ways the Kennedys were that same wholesome, ideal family that seemed too good to be true. But for how long? How much longer before Grant issued an ultimatum and all illusions were shattered?

"I'm glad Audrey finally fell asleep in the other room," Trish said. "She's always so wound up this time of year, it's enough to drive me crazy. Santa Claus and ho, ho, ho and all that sugar Mom feeds us doesn't help much."

"Yum, fudge. Right up there with her pastries. I'll have to go on a diet to fit into my new ted—"

Cammie stopped suddenly, strangely shy in spite of Trish's discovery and acceptance.

"Your *what*? Spill it, Cammie. Grant gave you a teddy, didn't he? And not of the bear variety, I'll bet."

"It's black satin and lace," she admitted, the feel of it beneath her dorm shirt seductively wicked against her skin. "He gave me some diamond earrings to wear with it."

"Something tells me it's not the only diamond you'll get this year."

Propping herself up on an elbow, Cammie gazed seriously at Trish's beautiful, animated face. "I'm afraid of dividing the family. You're not nearly as conservative as Mom and Dad are, Trish. They took me in, they never held anything back. I just can't bear the thought of jeopardizing their sense of stability by giving Grant the total commitment he wants. And deserves."

"It's a tough row to hoe, Sis. And you're the only one who can make that decision."

She sighed. "I know. And I just keep putting it off. Like the problem's actually going to go away. Grant says I'm afflicted with something called the Ostrich Syndrome."

"He's getting impatient, isn't he?"

"You know him as well as I do."

Trish chuckled. "Not quite. And speaking of impatient, I'll bet he's wondering what's keeping you."

Cammie shot her a sharp glance. "What makes you think that?"

"Oh, get real, Cammie. You're just waiting for me to fall asleep to sneak in there. The same as I used to do when Mark and I were engaged and he slept in the den."

"Grant and I aren't engaged. And besides, our circumstances aren't exactly the same."

"So what? Would you rather gab with me all night, or cuddle up to your honey?"

They could get caught, Cammie thought, but not likely. It meant a lot to Grant—as it did to her. Yes, it would be a step forward. Not an easy one, but a commitment they both needed. They seemed to be stuck at a plateau, and it was either go forward or retreat.

Swinging her legs over the side of the bed, Cammie got up. Her heart was beating fast and her steps were slow. But she took them just the same.

Pausing at the door, she whispered, "Thanks for the nudge, Trish. And for understanding."

"Sure, Sis. Sleep tight." As the door quietly shut, Trish's smile disappeared, and she muttered sadly, "Lord, I need a life again too."

Looking anxiously in all directions, Cammie walked quickly down the hall, careful to avoid the squeaking board to the right of Grant's room. The door was cracked open, and she pushed it in. The small "creak" sounded loud as an alarm, giving her away, she thought apprehensively.

She quickly slipped into the room and closed the door. The clicking of the lock was magnified in the stillness. While her eyes adjusted to the darkness, she made her way toward the direction of his voice.

"I knew you'd come," he whispered, and she could see him push back the covers, extend his hand. She stopped beside the bed's edge, then dropped the dorm shirt to the floor.

His low, sensual murmur of pleasure reached out of the dark and brought her into his open arms. The bed was warm from his body, a bed she had seen him sleeping in since his youth. But he was naked, already hard. This was a man who knew her body as well as his own, who whispered intimate words of love while he stripped her in the forbidden sanctuary of his family home.

What they were doing should be wrong, she told herself. Then why did their hands, caressing with a familiar, heated passion, seem to seal their destiny as never before?

In the pale moonlight, she gazed up at him as he mounted her. His eyes met hers with the intensity of purpose, and then he plunged into her. He entered her swift and deep, sinking to the mouth of her womb and claiming her in a way that was somehow different than ever before.

He raised up, poised, then thrust again.

"The bed," she whispered urgently at the give-away sound. "Grant, it's—"

Before she could protest, he maneuvered her to the floor with a quick, lithe silence. She felt the carpet against her cheek, her breasts, before he tucked a pillow beneath her head, then pushed another under her belly. With sure hands he lifted her hips, and drove himself into her contracting warmth again and again.

She couldn't see his face, but his roughly whispered words were potent, as was his driving need for possession. Haze was clouding her mind, but even so she suddenly understood the difference in their fevered lovemaking. He was taking her with a primal hunger that seemed to echo *possess . . . possess . . . possess.*

"You're mine," he said hoarsely before he pushed aside her hair and kissed her neck, roughly enough to leave a telltale mark. Would anyone see his mark? She didn't know and she didn't care. All she could think of was the drugging sensation, the suction on her neck shooting down to her womb.

"Mine," he whispered when he lifted his mouth. "Now. Always. Everywhere. *Here*."

How long their bodies battled and loved, she wasn't sure. When she would have sobbed her shattering release, she bit her fist to keep from crying out. Grant groaned into her hair, then collapsed over her body, his chest slick with the exertion.

He rolled off her and gathered her into his arms. Exhausted, she rested her head on his chest. They lay silent, spent, then he lifted her onto the bed.

"I love you," he murmured. "With my whole soul, I love you."

She sought his eyes, sensing a difference. Something had emerged in him that hadn't been there before she'd entered his room.

Or maybe it was in her. She had come there with misgivings, but now that she should go, more than anything she wanted to stay and never leave. She was bound to him, his woman and mate. It was wrong to sleep apart after forging a completion that went beyond words.

"You're my life, Grant. I don't think I could live without you."

He kissed her tenderly. "Cammie, I want to—"

The sound of the bathroom door closing interrupted him, and she tensed before she could stop herself.

Grant muttered a low curse.

Anxious to grab back the magic, she made her body relax into his. "Yes, Grant. You want to what?"

Sighing heavily, he pushed back her tangled hair. "I just wanted to wish you a Merry Christmas."

Thirteen

Grant looked at his new watch. Eleven-forty. He glanced across the room at Cammie, who gave the impression of listening attentively to Aunt Mabel, who was probably recounting her recent battle with gout. He felt the acceleration of his heart.

Resting against it was The Ring, tucked securely into the breast pocket of his suit jacket. His face was set in determination as he continued to stare at Cammie . . . and remembered their coupling. Taking her here, in this house on Christmas Eve, had turned the tide. He had branded her as his, with passion and fury and in defiance of parental morality.

Whether it was a conscious decision or not, Cammie had thrown her lot in with his that night, giving him the pledge of loyalty he'd sought from the very beginning.

Her mouth moved as she managed to get a word in edgewise, while her eyes scanned the New Year's Eve crowd. They locked with his.

With a slight inclination of his head, he indicated the front porch. She nodded, her lips curving in an inviting, intimate smile.

Grant patted the ring in his pocket, then moved purposefully in their agreed direction. He cherished their silent language, so well understood with no more than a look, a small gesture.

He beat her there, which wasn't surprising, considering Aunt Mabel's fondness for discussing her health. And it was fine, since he could use a few minutes alone, away from the crowd of friends and relatives. He knew what he wanted to say, and in case she put up a valiant last stand, his counterargument was ready.

Still, his palms were sweating; his heart was beating as though he'd just run a marathon. This would be one of the most important moments of his life, a moment that would change their future forever.

The front door opened. The noise of revelry spilled out before it shut again, leaving her footsteps on the wood and his erratic breathing the only sounds.

Stepping out of the shadows, he said, "Cammie. Here."

She crossed the narrow porch to where he stood near the side. They were alone, though New Year's toasts and blowing horns intruded faintly from inside.

Wordlessly, she walked into his arms and kissed him full upon the mouth.

"I've missed you tonight," she murmured, loving the feel of his hands on her waist. "All those people, when I only want to be with you."

Reluctantly, she moved back to lean against a porch post, just in case someone decided he or she, too, needed a breath of fresh air. Grant stepped closer and braced his elbow above her head.

"Do you?" he asked. "Want to be only with me?"

She touched his cheek, his jaw, all of him so wonderfully male. He moved his lips into her palm, pressing a moist, lingering kiss there.

"You're the only man I could ever want, Grant." She smiled with a sensual longing. "Let's make our excuses and go home, as soon as we see the New Year in. I'll follow you in my car and we can have our own private celebration." With a conspiratory wink she added, "I even left my keys in the ignition for a quick getaway, in case we decided to neck in the backseat."

Grant didn't return her smile. His eyes were somber, his expression serious.

"I'd like to celebrate more than New Year's, Cammie. I want to start the rest of our lives together." He reached into his pocket and held a ring up in the moonlight. The simple diamond-and-gold band glinted a sparkling promise.

She had known it was coming, yet she wasn't prepared. She wasn't ready for this, not yet, not here.

"That's Grandmother's wedding ring," she whispered, her voice catching, her heart racing, dread and excitement blending uneasily.

"She gave it to me just before she died. She made me promise to choose carefully and to love whoever wore it as much as she loved Granddad. 'Make sure it's for life,' she said. I gave her my word. And I plan to keep it."

"But, Grant, that's Mom's mother. What if she can't accept this? How can I wear her mother's ring if she's against us?" Cammie was grasping at straws and finding none. There was only the unwavering strength of his love opposing the glaring realities she had dodged, and that were now staring her straight in the face.

"Then that's her problem. Grandmother gave it to me, nobody else. It's my decision—*our* decision. I'm asking you to marry me, Cammie. I want you to wear this ring, to be my wife. I want to have children, and teach them that real love has no boundaries. Then one day when we're gone, one of them will have this ring and know that what matters most in life sometimes comes with a price. From us they'll learn the meaning of loyalty, devotion, and, yes, even sacrifice." He brought her hand to his mouth and kissed her ring finger. "Marry me. Love me enough to risk it."

Her heart swelled with love for him, yet she was torn.

"I *do* love you, Grant. I love you more than life, more than any woman should have the right to love a man. But, please, Grant. I beg you, just a little more time. Three months, you promised. And in my mind, I know I'm guilty of holding out, of waiting to be as strong about this as you. Give me just a few more weeks, and I swear I'll reconcile what's tearing me up right now. Give us that long to talk to our parents. Just a few more weeks before we take the final step."

Her eyes beseeched him. She pressed the ring between their palms. It felt warm from the heat of his body, charged with electric emotion. "Please," she whispered.

"No." He pushed away from the post, then drew her insistently against him. "If you love me the way you say you do, there's only one decision you can make, no matter what happens as a result."

In the background a loud chorus chanted: *TEN . . . NINE . . . EIGHT . . .*

"Time's out, Cammie. I want your answer. And I want it now."

He locked her against him, one hand tangled in her hair, the ring pressed into the small of her back from the pressure of his other palm.

"Kiss me," he whispered, his voice husky with need and demand. "Kiss me at midnight, and face our fate."

. . . FOUR . . . THREE . . .

His mouth fit over hers, seeking and hot. Knowing only that she loved him, that she couldn't live without him, she responded from the deepest depths of emotion and physical yearning. She craved his mouth, she came home within the hollow of his heart. Her body arched into his as she sought to bond the cradle of her feminine warmth to the hard, uncompromising strength of his maleness.

"HAPPY NEW YEAR! 'Should auld acquaintance be forgot and never brought to mind . . .'"

Wrapped in the haven of ecstasy, she wasn't aware of the door opening, the revelers spilling out.

"'Should auld acquaintance be—'"

The words died to a whisper; gasps of shock rippled through the crowd. Grant and Cammie broke apart as their family swelled onto the porch. It was all unreal and too very real. Cammie couldn't think. Her mind was jerking in all directions, taking it in, rejecting what was happening, only to be quickly throttled with the reality of the nightmare.

"Just what the hell is going on!" Edward bellowed. "Grant! Cammie! For the love of heaven—"

"Oh my God," Dorothy gasped, staggering back against her husband as though dealt a bodily blow.

Cammie looked from one stricken face to another, the scene unfolding with a slow, inevitable horror. No, it couldn't be like this . . . They were going to talk, make everything miraculously all right so she could keep the only man she'd ever love and the only family she'd ever belong to.

"No," she cried, her fist against her mouth. "No!"

And then she was running from it, turning her back on the horrible menagerie of gawking faces, the obscene spectacle of their outrage and disbelief.

She didn't feel the ground beneath her flying feet. Her eyes were unseeing as she grappled with numb fingers to turn the key in the ignition.

She kept trying to run from the nightmare, her foot pressing urgently down on the gas pedal. If only she could block it all out, but she couldn't. Couldn't think past the terrible thing she had just witnessed. It kept zooming in for a close-up, the camera of her mind refusing to edit the grotesque image she had played the leading role in. Oh, how she had hurt them, brutally, insensitively shredded their trust.

Get away . . . get away. This can't be real, her mind kept repeating, trying to salvage her tattered hope and love.

Somehow she made it home. Home to where Grant shared her bed.

Grant. Oh, God, what had she done? She'd left him there alone to face them. Alone with his ring.

In that moment she hated herself. She hated her cowardice, her damnable fear of commitment. Grant had been right all along.

Her legs could barely support her, she was shaking so bad. Stumbling, she made her way to the tiny bar in her living room, knocking glasses over in her unsteady haste.

A drink. For the first time in her life she needed a drink. Something strong enough to clear her head, because she felt more drunk than sober. Only she wasn't seeing pink elephants. All she could see was what she'd left behind: Edward outraged. Dorothy looking as though she would faint. Grant . . . Oh dear Lord, she could still hear him calling her name, asking her to stop.

She hadn't. She'd run like a frightened child, or an idiot who didn't have the courage to fight for the right to love, to stand beside a man who would move heaven and earth to claim her.

Think. Yes, she had to think. She couldn't even negotiate the liquor into the tumbler, so she drank greedily from the bottle. She didn't notice how the brandy burned down her throat, or seeped from the sides of her mouth and trickled onto her dress. Why should she notice? Why should she care?

The bottle slid from her nerveless fingers, and she crumpled onto the floor, burying her face in her hands.

Why had she run? Because she'd been running all her life. But if only she had quit when Grant had insisted—at the beginning, the day at the cottage—none of this would have happened. She'd created the mess and left him behind to clean it up.

He had every right never to forgive her for what she'd done. She had to find him, tell him she was wrong, so terribly wrong. But she was drunk now, she couldn't drive. She could hardly pick herself off the floor, so she crawled to the phone. Fumbling with the buttons, she somehow managed to get the number right.

His machine answered, his deep, vibrant voice sending memories on a rampage, the tears at last springing to life and rolling down her cheeks.

"Grant, please if you're there, answer me. Come home," she sobbed. "I'm sorry. So sorry. Come back and I'll make it up to you. I'll marry you—"

The beep cut her off.

Marriage. Oh, Lord, what had she done? He had to think she'd refused him. Would he come after her? Would he come to berate her and demand she prove she still deserved his love? Surely he would, surely . . .

She dissolved into drunken, hysterical tears, the phone dangling limply in her hand as she curled into the fetal position and wept.

Finally darkness claimed her, and she knew only the old dreams of a highway massacre blending into the even bigger loss of her own making.

Was it the pounding in her head that woke her, or the light seeping through the window?

Cammie pried her swollen eyes open. The escape of sleep had deserted her, and now she had only the blaring reality of day.

She sat up, hung over, disoriented. Everything came back into focus with hideous clarity. Grant's proposal, the scene, her flight.

And now. Alone. Grant hadn't come after all. The phone receiver still lay on the floor, and she dropped it back into its cradle. Then she stared at it, snatched it back up frantically, and dialed his number once more.

His machine answered. He wasn't home. Or he was refusing to listen. She left another message.

Gathering herself off the floor, she moved on stiff legs, heedless of her stained and rumpled dress. She knew what she had to do. She had to find him. Beg his forgiveness, then vow her eternal commitment to him, and only to him. She would promise to face their parents. Alone, if that's what he wanted.

Anything. Everything. She would stop at nothing to prove she deserved what he had offered.

Cammie got into her car, shuddering at the memory of her urgent escape in it not ten hours before. It couldn't have been so short a time since her life had changed forever, since she had finally understood that her words weren't hollow, that she couldn't live without him, no matter what the price.

His car wasn't in his driveway, but she let herself into the house to look for any sign that he had been there, had gotten her message and had chosen to turn her away for once.

The signal light was on, and she depressed the "play" button. Her voice flailed her, raw, broken, sobbing, too vivid. After the playback, she shut her eyes. With resolution, she played it again . . . and again. Then left it.

If he came home, she wanted him to hear. That was her. Stripped of all dignity, emotionally naked, and pleading. It was her recompense, her entreaty.

Scribbling a quick note, her hands trembling, she wrote her destination, her intent, and a final proclamation of commitment.

Back in her car, she squared her shoulders, then set out to do what she should have done months before. The miles slid away beneath the tires and she was anxious but strangely calm as she neared the place where she had disgraced herself and betrayed something more than her parents' trust.

She'd betrayed Grant's love, his trust. As well as her own.

The Kennedys' driveway was deserted, except for

the family sedan. Getting out of the car, she glanced down at herself and noticed her disheveled appearance for the first time—and didn't care. Determined to right her wrongs, she took a deep breath, said a silent prayer, and knocked twice on the door.

She might not be welcome. She might not be considered family anymore. And so she waited, like some stranger who couldn't enter without invitation.

The door suddenly opened, and she stood face-to-face with Dorothy.

"May I come in?" she asked quietly, meeting Dorothy's eyes without flinching, eyes that were as red and puffy as her own.

Dorothy swung the door all the way open. "Why did you knock, sweetheart? The door was unlocked."

Sweetheart? Not traitor, incestuous fornicator, the moral compromiser of her only son?

"I didn't think I'd be welcome," Cammie said uncertainly, trying hard not to hope for too much, not to cry out her relief that she wasn't shunned.

"Not welcome?" Dorothy exclaimed. "How could you not be welcome? You're our daughter."

She opened her arms with maternal acceptance. Cammie took one halting step forward, then another. And then she was being embraced with the unconditional acceptance she had always longed for, had always tried so hard to earn.

But it had been there for the taking all along, without conditions or reserve.

"Oh, Mom," she cried, clinging tight. "Mom, I'm so sorry. I didn't mean to hurt you or disgrace you. I couldn't help it. We're in love. So much in love."

"There now," Dorothy soothed, urging her toward the kitchen. "Dad's in here and we're going to have a little talk. We're sorry we drove you away, the way we acted. But it was such a—a shock, Cammie. You should have told us."

"I was afraid to," she said, swiping away tears of relief. "I didn't think you'd approve . . . and Grant . . . he wanted to be honest with you from the beginning. But I was too much of a coward. I couldn't bear to think of losing you and Dad."

"Nonsense," Edward boomed as he joined them at the kitchen table. He took Cammie's free hand; Dorothy was holding tight to the other. "I admit it's not exactly an easy thing for Mom and me to accept. But we'll get used to it. What's important is, that you and Grant do the right thing."

"We're getting married. At least, if he'll still have me after I deserted him, we will."

"Of course he'll still have you," Dorothy assured her. "He loves you very much, Cammie. He told us about it before he left last night."

"Do you know where he is?" she asked anxiously. "I've looked for him, I've called him. He never went home."

Dorothy and Edward exchanged a worried look.

"He was pretty upset when he left. We tried to get him to stay, but he said he wanted to be alone."

"We thought he'd drive over to check on you and let you know everything was going to be okay."

"Do you think he's hurt? Or—or—" She couldn't bring herself to say it. "He drives so fast, it scares me."

Edward and Dorothy didn't dispute her, their silence heightening her anxiety.

"I'll get in my car and drive around to see if I can find him," Edward said.

"I'll call Trish and ask if he's been by her."

Cammie almost knocked her chair over in her urgency to help.

"I'll backtrack to his house," she said, "and—Oh, no. I forgot to leave a message at my place. I've got to get home, or he'll think the worst."

"Cammie, sweetheart, I don't think you're in any condition to drive. You look like you need some tending."

She stopped at the front door just long enough to reassure Dorothy that she was fine. "And besides, I have to do *something*. I'm worried sick about him, Mom."

"He'll be fine," Dorothy said, though her expression of concern didn't match her confident voice. "The good Lord will watch after him. But if you're determined to go, promise me you'll watch after yourself. There are a lot of drunk drivers on the road on New Year's."

"I promise." Cammie kissed her quickly, then embraced Edward before he could hurry to his own car.

"We love you, Cammie," Dorothy said. "Nothing could ever make us stop."

"I know that now, Mom, Dad. I only wish I'd realized it sooner."

"Hindsight's twenty-twenty vision," Edward said. "The main thing is that you make the most of the future."

"I will," she vowed. "As soon as I find Grant."

Fourteen

The phone rang the second she opened the door. Cammie ran to answer it, almost tripping over her own feet to get there.

"Grant!" she said breathlessly, hoping against hope it was he.

"Sorry, it's just me," Russ said, then coughed harshly. "Cammie, I'm really sick. I know I promised to sit in for you tonight but—" He hacked several more times, then sneezed. "Man, I feel awful. I'll never make it through the newscast."

"But, Russ, I can't. I mean, there's an emergency, and I—No. Someone else will have to do it."

"I already called the sta—" He stopped long enough to wheeze. "The sub's out of town till sometime tonight. She can make it for ten. But Jack's expecting you for the six o'clock—Ahh-choo! Ohh, crud. What's the emergency?"

"I can't find Grant."

"Oh. Hey, he'll show up. He's nuts about you."

And emotionally unhinged after she dumped on him, she added silently, and driving around in a dangerous car on New Year's Day.

171

She sighed heavily. "Okay, Russ. But just for the six o'clock report."

She was late. She knew Jack would be going into a tailspin, with her arriving just minutes before the countdown.

There'd been no sign of Grant. Dorothy and Edward had called the police while she'd phoned the hospitals. They were going to keep looking and phone her the second they found him.

"Jeez, Cammie, are you trying to give me heart failure?" Jack exclaimed when she entered the studio. "Get in that chair. You've got one minute to countdown, and . . . Brother, do you look terrible. What's going on? Too much of a good thing last night?"

"Hardly," she muttered. "Let's just get this show on the road so I can get out of here."

"We've got weather and sports covered, but otherwise, you're it," he informed her, half-running to his position while she rushed to hers.

"Ten . . . nine . . . eight . . ."

Jack's cue was an ominous reminder of the midnight countdown. Frantically she tried to clear her head of everything but the news—the news she hadn't had time to give so much as a preliminary glance.

"Three . . . two . . . one."

"Good evening, and happy New Year," she said automatically, grateful that her years as a pro enabled her to wing it. Depending heavily on the TelePrompTer, she made it through the headlines, fighting to keep her concentration.

At the first commercial break Jack gave her a thumbs-up sign. "You're doing great, Cammie. Keep it up."

"Thanks, Jack. Any phone calls for me while I was on the air?"

"No, but we got a message that the Minicam's on its way with a cameraman to cover a bad accident. We'll have to squeeze the news flash in at the end, if he gets there in time."

"Any details?" she asked anxiously.

"Not yet. He'll call us on the car phone to give us the details and patch in with the visual while you announce. Sorry, but you already know we've got a shortage of reporters. Uh-oh, countdown. Hang in there, Cammie."

A terrible sense of foreboding gripped her. Somehow she got through the second portion without any major foul-ups, then turned it over to the sports and weather announcers. A chill grew inside her as she waited for Jack to run to the control booth as the anticipated call came through.

Haunting visions of her family seared her mind while she told herself it was nothing. She always tensed up whenever she reported on accidents. Yes, that was it. She was just upset because of that. Nothing out of the ordinary. Nothing to be alarmed about—

Jack interrupted her frantic attempts at rationalization. He pushed some notes into her clammy hands just before the final commercial break rolled to a close. He pointed out the crucial points to cover, then scooted away just before he signaled her that she was on.

For a horrifying moment she stared woodenly at the camera.

"This just in," she said faintly as Jack waved his hands in a frantic gesture for her to get going. Cammie gulped hard and forced the words out in a strained, high-pitched voice.

"A tragic New Year's accident involving two Porsche sports cars has claimed the life of a local man, whose identity is being withheld pending notification of relatives. The fate of the driver of the second car is not known at the moment." Jack indicated that the Minicam was patched in, and she stared sightlessly at the screen. At Grant's mutilated automobile, at the macabre activity surrounding it.

"One car is currently—" Her voice caught. "Is currently being attended by rescue workers, where the jaws of life are hard at work in an attempt to—to extricate the body of a man pinned inside the car's crushed remains. At this time, the state of his condition is unknown."

Jack indicated that the camera was once again focused on her. She made herself face the lens, the thousands of invisible viewers, as her world crumbled around her.

She was visibly shaking from head to toes, her voice toneless. "We'll bring you up-to-date with the situation on the ten o'clock report. This is Cammie Walker saying—good night."

The cameras cut off immediately. Jack rushed over to her.

"Good Lord, Cammie, what is going on?"

"Grant," she whispered. "Grant." She stared at Jack in a state of shock. "I have to go to him."

"That was your brother? Oh, Jeez, Cammie, I didn't know, I didn't—"

"Not my brother. My lover. My fiancé."

"Which one?" he said quickly. "Which—"

"I don't know. I don't—"

Could he have survived? Could he still be alive in that horrible-looking wreckage? Could he be the one survivor? Still in a state of shock, she grabbed her purse, then ran for the exit. Jack was fast on her heels.

She stopped at the door just long enough to

demand, "Where? Where is he? I don't know where to—"

"You're in no condition to drive. I've got the location. C'mon, honey, I'll get you there as fast as I can. It's close by."

Was it for minutes or hours that she stared almost comatose out the window as Jack sped to the accident scene? She didn't cry. She was beyond tears. She didn't hear Jack's voice as he attempted to console her. She heard only Grant's voice calling her name, telling her to stop, to come back.

And then they were there, amidst the frenzied activity surrounding a horribly damaged sports car. She saw an ambulance, police cars, rescue workers and paramedics, curious spectators . . . and blood. The smell of it, and of death, tainted the air. She almost expected to see the bodies of her family—but she was looking for Grant's body.

She'd thought she was healed. She'd thought, with the help of Grant's love and care, she'd put all of her guilt behind her. But she hadn't, for here she was again—a fatal car accident . . . their fight . . . her fault . . .

Trembling, wild with fear and rage at herself, she stumbled out of Jack's car and toward the Porsche that the rescue workers were frantically working on. Grant, she thought numbly. He had to be alive. He had to be. . . .

She glanced at the other Porsche, empty, strangely lethal looking, even when motionless and all but destroyed by the crash. The driver's door was horribly smashed, thrusting into the interior of the car.

. . . *claimed the life of a local man* . . .

Suddenly the other Porsche burst into flames. The rescue workers and onlookers scurried to safety, but Cammie started running toward the blazing corpse of metal.

"Grant!" she screamed over and over again.

Unseen hands grabbed her, jerked her to a stop. She struggled against their hold.

"I see him, Cammie! I see him!" Jack shook her until she quit flailing against him, then pushed her toward the median strip.

She took a few steps forward, then stopped, staring at the man sitting there.

Grant. Blood covered his face and arms, dripped in dark rivers over his ragged clothing. His head was bowed, his arms dangling loose between his legs.

"Grant," she whispered, then cried, "Grant!"

She raced to him and, her entire body shaking, knelt beside him. He didn't look up, didn't move. Where were the medics? she wondered. Why weren't they taking care of him? She touched him gingerly, his arms, his legs, not wanting to hurt him more. He didn't seem to have broken bones, but the blood—

Moving closer, she looked into his eyes—the eyes of a man in deep shock, who didn't know where he was or what had happened. The blood seemed to come from small cuts and a few gashes on his face and arms. But he was all right.

She sobbed her heartache and joy while she carefully pressed hungry kisses over his battered face.

"Grant, can you see me? Can you look at me?"

Searching his face, desperate for any sign that he recognized her, she prayed . . . and watched with speechless gratitude to God as awareness dawned in the eyes of the man she loved so much.

"Oh, God, thank you." She wept. She clasped one of his hands, which, strangely, was clenched into a fist. She kissed it over and over, then gently pried it open.

The ring fell onto the ground, released from his convulsive grasp.

She grabbed it, held it tight. "Grant, I love you. Look at me. Just look at me."

His eyes opened farther. She held the ring up and saw him focus on it.

"I told Mom and Dad, Grant. I told them how much I love you and that I was going to marry you."

She lifted her left hand and slid the ring down her finger.

"With this ring, I thee wed. For richer or poorer, in sickness and in health, till—"

Her voice caught. "Forgive me, Grant. Forgive me for running away. I promise I'll always be there from now on, no matter what. I love you. *I love you.*" She sobbed, clasping his hand again.

Slowly, faintly, he smiled. Then, as if with his last bit of strength, he spoke. "I . . . love . . . you."

Epilogue

When they entered the church foyer, Cammie
smelled the perfume of orange blossoms and gar-
denias. The organist played sweetly in the background. The low murmur of whispers from the
filled pews fell softly upon her ears.

"God be with you," Dorothy whispered before an
usher escorted her down the aisle.

"My sister," Trish murmured as she handed
Cammie a white Bible and a spray of springtime
flowers. She hugged her, and then, as the organist
struck the first notes of the processional, started
slowly down the aisle.

Audrey, looking slightly confused despite the
previous night's rehearsal, tugged at Cammie's
hand and said too loudly for the occasion, "Gee,
Aunt Cammie, you sure do look pretty today."

"Thank you, Audrey. You're pretty as a bride
yourself." Cammie smiled nervously while Audrey
grinned and swung her basket of rose petals, then
skipped down the aisle behind her mother.

Edward hugged Cammie close and tucked her

trembling hand into the crook of his arm. "Ready?" he asked, a twinkle in his eye. "They're playing our song . . . daughter."

They walked down the aisle, Cammie's heart swelling until she thought it might burst. Her misting gaze locked with Grant's as he watched her from the front of the church, his eyes reflecting devotion and desire. He wore charcoal-gray pants and a morning coat, a gray and white ascot over a pristine white shirt. She couldn't imagine a more handsome and loving bridegroom.

As she and Edward neared the altar, Grant stepped forward to meet them. His and Cammie's love, he thought, was as miraculous as his surviving the deadly car crash. He knew his mother gave credit to heavenly intervention, which he was certain had a lot to do with it. But looking at Cammie now—a vision in white, the diamond-and-aquamarine pins gleaming in her hair, matched by her locket and diamond earrings—he knew miracles began on earth.

He didn't remember much about the accident itself, only his desolation, his sense of loss. But then she had come for him, and he'd been determined to claim their destiny.

His dad moved aside, allowing Grant to take his rightful place. Edward sat in the front pew and wrapped his arm around Dorothy's shoulders. Their faces beamed with joy and pride. Trish exchanged a flirtatious smile with Grant's best man. Audrey stepped on the hem of her gown and littered the floor with the few petals she hadn't already strewn.

Grant kissed Cammie's hand, then held it tight. They moved as one to the altar, and bowed their heads in unison.

Their vows began, the ones they had written

together with great care. They recited their declaration of loyalty and commitment, and acknowledged how fragile life was, how precious a gift love was.

The resonant voice of the good reverend concluded, "Ladies and gentlemen, I present to you, Mr. and Mrs. Grant Kennedy."

They proudly faced the audience as husband and wife.

"Grant," she whispered, "My husband."

"My wife," he murmured, then gathered her into both arms to seal their vows with a lingering kiss.

THE EDITOR'S CORNER

What a joy it is to see, hear, smell and touch spring once again! Like a magician, nature is pulling splendors out of an invisible hat—and making us even more aware of romance. To warm you with all the radiance and hopefulness of the season, we've gathered together a bouquet of six fabulous LOVESWEPTs.

First, from the magical pen of Mary Kay McComas, we have **KISS ME, KELLY,** LOVESWEPT #462. Kelly has a rule about dating cops—she doesn't! But Baker is a man who breaks the rules. In the instant he commands her to kiss him he seizes control of her heart—and dares her to tell him she doesn't want him as much as he wants her. But once Kelly has surrendered to the ecstasy he offers, can he betray that passion by seducing her to help him with a desperate, dirty job? A story that glows with all the excitement and uncertainties of true love.

With all things green and beautiful about to pop into view, we bring you talented Gail Douglas's **THE BEST LAID PLANS,** LOVESWEPT #463. Jennifer Allan has greenery *and* beauty on her mind as she prepares to find out exactly what Clay Parrish, an urban planner, intends to do to her picturesque hometown. Clay is a sweet-talker with an irrepressible grin, and in a single sizzling moment he breaches Jennifer's defenses. Once he begins to understand her fears, he wages a glorious campaign to win her trust. A lot of wooing . . . and a lot of magic—in a romance you can't let yourself miss.

In Texas spring comes early, and it comes on strong—and so do the hero and heroine of Jan Hudson's **BIG AND BRIGHT,** LOVESWEPT #464. Holt Berringer is one of the good guys, a long lean Texas Ranger with sin-black eyes and a big white Stetson. When the entrancing spitfire Cory Bright has a run-in with some bad guys, Holt admires her refusal to hide from threats on her life and is determined to cherish and protect her. Cory fears he will be too much like the domineering macho men she's grown to dislike, but Holt is as tender as he is tough. Once Cory proves that she can make it on her own, will she be brave enough to settle for the man she really wants? A double-barreled delight from the land of yellow roses.

Peggy Webb's **THAT JONES GIRL,** LOVESWEPT #465, is a marvelous tale about the renewal of an old love between a wild Irish rover and a beautiful singer. Brawny wanderer Mick Flannigan had been Tess Jones's first lover, best friend, and husband—until the day years before when he suddenly left her. Now destiny has thrown them together again, but Tess is still too hot for Mick to handle. She draws him like a magnet, and he yearns to recapture the past, to beg Tess's forgiveness . . . but can this passion that has never died turn into trust? For Peggy's many fans, here is a story that is as fresh, energetic, and captivating as a spring morning.

Erica Spindler's enchanting **WISHING MOON,** LOVESWEPT #466, features a hero who gives a first impression that belies the real man. Lance Alexander seems to be all business, whether he is hiring a fund-raiser for his favorite charity or looking for a wife. When he runs into the cocky and confident Madi Muldoon, she appears to be the last person he would choose to help in the fight to save the sea turtles—until she proves otherwise and he falls under the spell of her tawny-eyed beauty. Still Lance finds it hard to trust in any woman's love, while Madi thinks she has lost her faith in marriage. Can they both learn that wishes made on a full moon—especially wishes born of an irresistible love for each other—always come true? A story as tender and warm as spring itself.

In April the world begins to move outdoors again and it's time to have a little fun. That's what brings two lovers together in Marcia Evanick's delightful **GUARDIAN SPIRIT,** LOVESWEPT #467. As a teenager Josh Langly had been the town bad boy; now he is the local sheriff. When friends pair him with the bewitching dark-haired Laura Ann Bryant for the annual scavenger hunt, the two of them soon have more on their minds than the game.

Forced by the rules to stay side by side with Josh for a weekend, Laura is soon filled with a wanton desire for this good-guy hunk with the devilish grin. And though Josh is trying to bury his bad boy past beneath a noble facade, Laura enchants him beyond all reason and kindles an old flame. Another delectable treat from Marcia Evanick.

And (as if this weren't enough!) be sure not to miss three unforgettable novels coming your way in April from Bantam's spectacular new imprint, FANFARE, featuring the best in women's popular fiction. First, for the many fans of Deborah Smith, we have her deeply moving and truly memorable historical **BELOVED WOMAN**. This is the glorious story of a remarkable Cherokee woman, Katherine Blue Song, and an equally remarkable frontiersman Justis Gallatin. Then, making her debut with FANFARE, Jessica Bryan brings you a spellbinding historical fantasy, **ACROSS A WINE-DARK SEA**. This story has already wowed *Rendezvous* magazine, which called Jessica Bryan "a super storyteller" and raved about the book, describing it as "different, exciting, excellent . . ." The critically-acclaimed Virginia Brown takes readers back to the wildest days of the Wild West for a fabulous and heartwarming love story in **RIVER'S DREAM**.

All in all, a terrific month of reading in store for you from FANFARE and LOVESWEPT!

Sincerely,

Carolyn Nichols

Carolyn Nichols,
Publisher,
LOVESWEPT
Bantam Books
666 Fifth Avenue
New York, NY 10103

NEW!
Handsome Book Covers Specially Designed To Fit Loveswept Books

Our new French Calf Vinyl book covers come in a set of three great colors—royal blue, scarlet red and kachina green.

Each 7" × 9½" book cover has two deep vertical pockets, a handy sewn-in bookmark, and is soil and scratch resistant.

To order your set, use the form below.